"I'm good enough to sleep with, but not good enough to marry?"

Blake's voice was low, growling at her.

Tension filled every atom of Crystal's body. "Are you asking for marriage?"

"No," he replied.

She relaxed. Even though she knew it sounded wrong, she had to do what was best for her. No one else would. "You and I both know we're not meant for marriage. But there's this chemistry thing..."

"Let me get this straight," he said. "After last night, you're saying you like me for a stud, but not for the long term."

"That's a coarse way of putting it, but yes."

His slow grin was as wolfish as it was sexy. "Well, then—" He pulled her toward him. "You can't complain if I take my job seriously."

With her hands on his nape she drew his mouth down to hers. "Okay, but you'd better be good, Blake. We've only got four more weeks until I go back to Santa Fe, so we have to make this relationship *very* memorable."

Rita Clay Estrada is a vibrant fixture in the world of romance writing. Not only has she written thirty-five novels to date, she created and co-founded the Romance Writers of America, the only organization of its kind in the world.

Early on, Rita established herself as a bestselling Harlequin Temptation author. Her stories always seem to strike the right emotional chord and fans won't be disappointed by *Million Dollar Valentine*. Newcomers to Rita Clay Estrada's work and loyal readers alike will welcome another "keeper" to the shelf.

Throughout her almost two decades as a prolific writer, Rita has also worked at a dizzying array of jobs. This year, she's studying to become an insurance appraiser on disaster sites! Rita raised her family in Texas and still lives in Houston.

Books by Rita Clay Estrada

HARLEQUIN TEMPTATION
450—ONE MORE TIME
474—THE COLONEL'S DAUGHTER
500—FORMS OF LOVE
518—THE TWELVE GIFTS OF CHRISTMAS
573—THE STORMCHASER
595—LOVE ME, LOVE MY BED
634—WISHES
687—DREAMS
713—EVERYTHING ABOUT HIM
733—ONE WILD WEEKEND

MillionDollar Valentine
Rita Clay Estrada

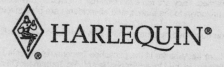

HARLEQUIN®

TORONTO • NEW YORK • LONDON
AMSTERDAM • PARIS • SYDNEY • HAMBURG
STOCKHOLM • ATHENS • TOKYO • MILAN • MADRID
PRAGUE • WARSAW • BUDAPEST • AUCKLAND

ISBN 0-373-25866-6

MILLION DOLLAR VALENTINE

Copyright © 2000 by Rita Clay Estrada.

Visit us at www.romance.net

Printed in U.S.A.

1

FROM THE expensive suit and the way he carried himself, the good-looking guy could have been a millionaire. From the frown, he looked like an uptight CEO. But, from the intense gaze of his penetrating deep-blue eyes, he resembled a lover.

An interesting...contradiction.

Clutching the to-do list her aunt had instructed her to follow before opening the flower and gift shop door, Crystal Tynan watched intently as he approached the shop's front door.

He stopped in the doorway, his very presence blocking all light. His suit was light-gray with a fine thread of blue woven through the material. His sandy-brown hair was thick and well cut. He had a strong face; nice cheekbones, a well-sculpted mouth and a great chin. His shoulders were broad, and the rest of him was just plain easy on the eyes, as Crystal's Aunt Helen would say. From her aunt's description, Crystal bet this was Blake Wright, manager of the Granite Run Mall just outside of Flagstaff, Arizona.

His midnight-blue eyes stared back, assessing and evaluating her just as intently. Although he wasn't returning her smile, he was interested, too, or he wouldn't be so focused. Either that or he was even more uptight than she'd first assumed.

It was two days after New Year's Day, and the mall would soon be as packed with shoppers as it had been during the holiday season—no doubt because of the after-holiday sales. This was Crystal's first day of filling in for her Aunt Helen and so far she hadn't accomplished more than two things on the list. Thank goodness the other employee—the one who knew how to run the store—would be in soon.

She placed the sheaf of papers on top of the glass showcase filled with small silver and gold trinkets, and held out her hand. "Hello, Blake Wright. It's so nice to meet the man my Aunt Helen loves."

He blinked twice, obviously not expecting that greeting. "I beg your pardon?"

Certainly he didn't take her literally. "Don't you manage this mall?"

"Yes." He sounded cautious as he took a few steps into the shop and faced her.

He was the right guy. She relaxed again. "Well, my aunt talks about you all the time."

Those wonderful blue eyes narrowed. Still no smile.

Obviously her aunt didn't talk about Crystal as much as she talked about him. Or—maybe he didn't understand her. After all, she *did* have a rather heavy East Texas drawl. "I'm Crystal Tynan," she said slowly and distinctly. "I'm here to manage the shop until Valentine's Day, while Aunt Helen recuperates from her broken arm."

Finally, recognition turned his eyes an iridescent blue. He took her hand in his. The tight look on his face slowly receded. "I'm glad you could make it," he said. "She was worried you wouldn't be able to get away from your, uh, job."

Crystal gave a light laugh, intrigued by the man. When his expression eased, he seemed like a different person. Although, if he was close enough to Aunt Helen to know Crystal had to get a release from her job to be here, he also knew what she did for a living. Some people were funny about masseuses. Occasionally, male clients came looking for more than just a massage, and she set them straight but fast.

Crystal smiled, pretending she had no doubts that he thought she was an upstanding citizen. "Since I'm a massage therapist, much of my income is based upon tips. I couldn't afford to lose out. Luckily, when my aunt broke her arm, the season was ending."

"I didn't know there was a season for massages." There was a dryness to his tone, but she ignored that, too. This time.

"There aren't for some. However, I work for a lodge during the ski season and that's very seasonal. And when the ski season is over, and before the spring tourist season begins, there are four or five dead weeks." She scraped back another strand of her hair, letting the full length of it fall over her shoulder and down her back. "Although, last year Santa Fe didn't have the normal lull between one season and the other. Everyone wants to visit."

"It's a beautiful city."

"And a very wealthy city," she added.

"Wealthy," he said slowly, paying such close attention to her mouth that her skin tingled. "Is that important?"

"Only if you're poor," she said with a straight face. Was he kidding? Usually only the wealthy asked silly questions like that.... "You don't happen to *own* this mall, do you?" she asked, pretending innocence.

He stayed serious. "No. Would it matter?"

She couldn't keep her smile away. "Probably a lot—to you."

Finally, Blake Wright smiled, too, and it was as if warm sunshine had flooded the flower shop. "I don't know about that. I don't have time to sit around and feel jealous for those who have more than I do. I enjoy what I have."

Her eyes widened. "I thank the powers that be for everything I have, too. But I'm certainly not silly enough to turn down more blessings—or money."

If she thought his smile was enticing, it was only because she hadn't heard his laughter—until now. It was deep and rich and wonderful, dancing down her spine and awakening each and every nerve in her body.

He really was a very handsome man. Out of her league, though. Darn.

"I have a feeling you make your own...blessings, Ms. Tynan," he finally answered.

"Please call me Crystal, and thank you for noticing. Yes, I do. I believe that if you don't go after what you want, you can't expect it to drop in your life. Just *saying* whatever you want isn't enough to make it happen."

"That's a go-getter philosophy," he teased. "I bet you get what you want a good fifty percent of the time."

She spotted the twinkle in his eye. "The odds had better be more than fifty percent."

"You're tough," he said, but there was a hint of admiration in his tone.

She smiled, soothed slightly by his compliment. "Thanks." For the first time she stepped away from the counter. "But not as tough as Aunt Helen will get if she finds out I haven't done right by her to-do list."

He gave an absent, "Mmm," and gave her a slow once-over.

Her casual black cotton blouse topped a red-black-brown-and-green full-tiered skirt that hung to her ankles. On her feet were doeskin soft moccasinlike boots dressed in fringe and silver, matching the conch leather belt cinching her waist. Then he noticed her fingers for the first time. A silver ring on every finger and both thumbs. Feather earrings hung to her shoulders.

"Goodness," he murmured.

She followed his gaze down her body to her skirt. "Colorful, isn't it?"

"All you need is a headband of beads and you'd look as if you'd time-warped from the sixties."

Somehow, his comment seemed a little stuffy. Instead, she smiled brightly. "Darn. I was going for the triumph over Custer look. Thank you. All that, and it's comfortable, too."

He frowned. "Is this the way they dress in Santa Fe?"

"Yes, only a little more casual." She glanced down at her list as if she were too busy to notice his frown. "But I dressed up for Flagstaff."

"Does Helen know?"

For just a fleeting moment, Crystal wanted to kick him in the shin. But with her boots on, it would hurt her as much as if she were barefoot. Instead, she turned and faced him directly, her gaze locking with his. "Aunt Helen isn't my mother. I'm a grown woman, Blake, in case you haven't noticed."

His gaze dropped immediately to her breasts and a small tickle of a smile edged his mouth before he looked back into her steady, brown-eyed gaze.

She waited a moment before continuing. "I choose my own clothes, friends and jobs. Now, if we have a problem with that, let's talk about it. Otherwise, I have work to do...." She waited for him to say something. But the female part of her couldn't help but wish he wasn't so handsome—especially when he was smiling.

"You're right and I apologize for talking out of turn," he said smiling slowly.

She could have been coy, or angry or any one of a hundred other emotions. She was none of those.

Instead, she placed a hand on his broad shoulder,

went up on her tiptoes and brushed his cheek with a butterfly kiss.

Then she stepped back. "My aunt would never forgive me if I didn't forgive you. And so, I accept your apology as long as you continue to wear that wonderful aftershave."

His blue eyes widened. "That's a sexist remark, Ms. Tynan. I would be accused of all kind of things if I said that to you."

"Yes, it is," she confirmed, still silently astounded at her own reaction to his nearness. "And, with you being so cute and all, if you said it to me about my perfume, I'd probably wear it again. However, not everyone is as open and honest as I am."

Blake laughed. "You're a lot like your Aunt Helen, do you know that?"

She smiled in satisfaction. "In other words, you can't get her to conform to your idea of what's right and what's not, either?" She gave a low chuckle. "Thank you for the compliment. It's one of the wonderful things that bond my aunt and I together. I want to be just like her when I grow up."

"I wouldn't doubt you'll succeed. Your chances are much better than fifty percent."

So he really *did* have a sense of humor. How delightful! "Tell me," she asked. "Are there any more like you at home who might have a million or two stashed away?"

"Nope. I'm the only child of a minister and his church secretary. No big money here." He looked at her quizzically. "Is a million important?"

"Oh, yes. Remember our discussion about money?" Crystal asked. "Well, if Aunt Helen had enough of it, she wouldn't need to bring me all the way from New Mexico. She could have hired someone locally to help her out. And I wouldn't have had to wait to come see her. I could have visited anytime."

Blake gave a chuckle and turned toward the door. "I wouldn't worry about your aunt's financial bottom line. Helen's got as much as she needs." When he reached the door, he gave her one more of "those" looks—the kind that said "you're out of my frame of reference, but you are still an intriguing woman." She'd seen "those" looks before. In fact, she'd given one or two to men in her twenty-six years.

"Don't take my concern wrong," she said softly. "I'm not the worrying kind."

"I didn't think so for a moment." He hesitated only a second or two. "Goodbye, Ms. Tynan," he stated formally.

"Goodbye, Blake," she stated informally.

Reluctantly, he continued on his way, but he gave one more sexy look over his shoulder before he left the shop.

Crystal took an extra moment to watch him walk through the mall toward his office. He had a nice walk, but it would have been more fun to watch him without his suit jacket on....

BLAKE FELT Crystal's eyes on him all the way down to the mall office. He was irritated, stimulated and self-conscious by that knowledge.

From the moment he'd seen Crystal Tynan, he'd been intrigued. Helen had called and told him this would be Crystal's first day and had asked him to welcome her, please. Instead, he'd forgotten what he went there for.

Crystal was a piece of work, he told himself, trying to minimize all the feelings he'd just gone through. That woman had gotten under his skin in less than a moment of not-too-close contact. By the time ten minutes had passed, he'd been intrigued in spite of himself.

She was very unlike the kind of woman he was usually drawn to. He liked a more chic appearance, a more conservative type of woman. This woman, though beautiful in her own way, looked like a free spirit. Not his type at all. To his mind, she was dressed all wrong for a store owner—especially for as elegant a shop as Helen's floral and gift shop. Although Flagstaff was part of the Southwest and many of the clerks dressed like Crystal, she was representing the owner. His friend.

He could have kicked himself for ignoring the real reason he'd wanted her dressed differently. He had to be honest. Her clothes were fine. He'd just wanted her to be a little more like him in her choice of clothing. Perhaps a little tailored. Maybe wearing high heels that gave the illusion of legs from here to there....

Where the hell did that thought come from? Blake

ditched that thought instantly, before he could react to the image.

Too late.

He wasn't looking for complications in his life right now. And Helen was just his friend, and all he needed to worry about was whether or not Crystal Tynan would maintain the shop's image and do the best job for Helen. The store wasn't called *Entrée* for nothing. It catered to Flagstaff's richest, most elite clientele, creating custom-designed floral arrangements and selling high-end unique gift items.

Wrong image or not, God she was beautiful. She had great hair. Taffy-colored, it sheered down her back almost touching her softly rounded hips. And those eyes. They were something. Big, uptilted, light and toasty-warm-brown and beautiful. A man could get lost in those eyes. He'd love to be looking down into them while... Squelch that thought, too. Reaching the office area of the mall, he opened the glass door and entered.

This was his favorite time of day. The mall held only employees and several mall-walkers, usually senior citizens who moved through in groups at a steady pace, enjoying the exercise as well as the controlled air-conditioning or heating. There weren't any problems—yet.

About an hour from now, many of the walkers would join together in one of the small lunch counters or eating establishments and have breakfast and lively talks.

By noon, the theater would open its doors and the

mall would be packed. Combine those two items with the after-holiday sales going on, and there would be chaos. He hoped Crystal could handle the crush.

"Hey, Marilyn," he said as he walked by his secretary's desk. An older woman, she was efficient and loyal. She'd been the mall's administrative secretary since the mall had opened over six years ago. He had inherited her, and he was damn lucky to have done so. "I'll be in my office for the next hour."

"Okay. Fresh coffee in the pot. Let me know if you need anything," she called, not bothering to look up. Instead, she continued going through the pile of mail stacked on top of her desk. She'd give him his portion later.

After he finished with the mail and before he had the meeting with the department store executives about the renovation plans, he might check and see how Crystal Tynan was doing. It was the prudent thing to do, seeing as she was new to the area and the business....

"AND THEN YOU CAN ADD one or two of these," Linda instructed, picking up several large orange silk flowers.

She looked up at Crystal as if she needed guidance, but pursed her lips to keep quiet. Linda was about ten years older than Crystal, half the height and twice the size—and just as sweet as could be.

A few customers wandered around the shop and both women had already approached them, but the lookers wanted to continue looking. Meanwhile, Crystal stood behind the counter while Linda demonstrated the basics of arranging.

Crystal took one stem, stood back and eyed the arrangement before carefully inserting the orange flower in the side center.

Linda smiled. "Very good," she said, pride evident in her voice as she praised her new student. "The symmetry is excellent."

"Thank you." Crystal gave a critical eye to the floral arrangement, then looked back at her teacher. "You really think so?"

"Definitely. It's very unusual, kinda like you, but it works. Kinda like..."

"I know," Crystal laughed. "Like me."

"Is that for sale?" one of the customers asked as she reached the counter with her purchases. It took Crystal a moment to realize she was talking about the arrangement.

"Oh, it's..." Linda began.

"It certainly is."

"How much?"

"Thirty-three dollars," Crystal announced calmly. "Marked down for the January sales."

The woman smiled. "I'll take it."

With an efficiency of movement, Linda took the woman's charge card and wrote up the item, then packed it carefully in wrap and bag. It wasn't until the woman left the store with her new purchase that both of them burst out laughing.

"Told you that it was unique. You've got talent," Linda said in satisfaction.

"That and thirty-three bucks will get you a floral arrangement from *Entrée*," Crystal stated in a low whisper. "Let's do one more before I take a break and stalk around the mall."

"You're on." Linda reached for another bowl, a brilliant purple one this time. "Get going, Ms. Tynan."

Crystal began choosing silk flowers from their holders, red, gold and a lighter purple; Mardi Gras colors. As she picked one, held it against the other and continued to choose, she decided it was about time to ask other questions. "Linda? What can you tell me about Blake Wright?" Not that she was interested. She was just curious. After all, she *should* be interested in her aunt's friend.

Linda pursed her lips thoughtfully, but there was a curious light in her eyes. "Well, he's the manager of this mall, and has been for two years. They brought him in from somewhere up north. He's thirty-something and strict on his rules and regulations about the mall. A little bit of a stuffed shirt, but the women don't seem to mind. And he used to date one of the buyers of the main department store here."

"Is she still in Flagstaff?"

"No, she was transferred." Linda frowned. "He didn't seem half as upset as she was, but you know how men are. When it comes to emotions, they never show anything."

Although a little on the shy side, Linda obviously held very firm opinions in a general kind of way. Especially about the male species.

"I don't run into too many men like that," Crystal murmured, sticking another flower into the wire cage at the bottom of the vase. "I work with a lot of guys who do nothing but moan about women all day long."

Linda's eyes widened, suspiciously. "Really?"

Nodding her head Crystal laughed.

They worked all morning, Crystal following Linda like a shadow as she learned the quirks and procedures of the shop and her Aunt Helen's way of doing business.

Having a myriad of jobs over the years made it easy to walk into a store and pick up the routine pretty quickly. Before she became a masseuse, she'd had a new job every quarter. It was fun. So was working in her aunt's shop. It wasn't for long, and then she'd be back at her own job and seeking the elusive millionaire who would fall in love and marry her, allowing her access to a whole new world.

Hers was a simple plan, really. She would enjoy her life to the fullest, trying all the things she wanted to try in her quest for the perfect career opportunity—something that would fill her days with challenge and laughter and money. Hard work and enjoyment went hand in hand to her way of thinking. She was willing to search for the finest of relationships, never settling for something less than the best.

She firmly believed that people made their own happiness. From what she'd seen, ninety percent of someone's happiness came from the mate that he or she chose. For her, the best relationships had to do with the right man. The second ingredient for happiness was money. With it, many of the everyday problems of life were solved before they began.

Ergo: she needed to fall in love and marry a millionaire who possessed a whole list of qualities Crystal required—trust, sense of humor, nice looks and a sense of adventure. And one who loved her as much as she loved him. That was a must.

How hard could that be? When working at the exclusive hotel, she was in the right business and the right place to meet wealthy businessmen. In fact, she'd met several, but, as of yet, not the right one. It wasn't that money was the only criteria. She needed more than money, but money was part of the equation. That sense of humor thing was really important, too. So was trust.

Keeping her goal of the perfect relationship in sight left all thoughts of entertaining a deeper relationship with Blake Wright out of her personal picture. He was sexy and handsome, but he wasn't wealthy. That meant she wouldn't look any further.

It wasn't that Blake wasn't worth a second look; it was that she had her heart set in a different direction. A different goal.

"Lunchtime," Linda said, touching her arm. "Shelly will be here in a few minutes to help cover for you. But if you want, why don't you go now and look around a little? We don't have any crunch to deal with right now."

"Thanks," Crystal said, reaching for her small, crocheted purse. Slinging it over her shoulder, she gave a wave and walked out.

Five minutes later, Crystal stared at the particularly unusual piece of art in a store window as she began walking away—only to walk right into Blake Wright's arms.

Her first reaction was a shiver of apprehension at the scent of danger.

Her second reaction was an exhilarating sense of delight.

But it wasn't the same reaction for Blake Wright. The handsome man was frowning down at her, his hands holding her arms as if they were iron railings and he was falling....

2

"WE'VE GOT to keep meeting like this," Crystal said, enjoying being in his arms even though his expression resembled a thundercloud. "I love surprises."

"You weren't looking where you were going." His frown made his thick, arched brows meet over the strong bridge of his nose.

And, of course she hadn't been watching, or she wouldn't be in his arms now. The way he said it, it sounded like an accusation. "No, I wasn't, was I?" she said brightly. "But I couldn't have planned it better if I'd tried."

"What?" If possible, the crease between his brows grew deeper.

"Well, I ran into the arms of a handsome man who is pure gentleman and with whom I'm safe."

He continued to frown. Where was this man's sense of humor? Apparently, her words didn't please him any more than her actions. "It could have been different."

Crystal gently pulled away. "But it wasn't," she reminded him firmly. "So I won't spend time worrying about what could have been."

He dropped his hands to his sides and she continued to walk. "Where are you going?"

Crystal raised her brows. "I beg your pardon?" It was her coolest voice, and it usually worked well with men in stalling any personal question.

It didn't seem to faze him. "It's lunchtime. Where are you going?"

"Eventually to the flower shop's back room. I have my own meal from home." She took another step back. "But right now, I'm walking the mall and checking out the window displays."

Blake hesitated a moment, and Crystal realized he didn't know quite what to say. She took pity on him. "Do you have a few minutes to walk along with me?"

He gave a quick nod. "A few. I'd like that."

Crystal pulled out a plastic sandwich bag from her purse and opened it, offering him a taste as if it were Godiva chocolate. "Would you like a carrot stick?"

"Carrot?" He peered inside the bag.

He couldn't be that ignorant. Carrots were good for a body, and he had to know that. "It won't hurt, I promise," she said, then something else caught her eye.

Her gaze rested on the next window. It was filled with young children's clothing; all the latest styles. She stopped and studied the bright colors, the way the mannequins had their soft cotton overall pant legs rolled, and the brilliant neon-colored buckets of sand for decoration. She forgot for a moment that he was standing by her side.

"Do you like children?" he asked, interrupting her thoughts.

She continued studying the window. "Love them. Especially if they belong to someone else and they're already little people, like these mannequins. See that tunnel?" she asked, pointing to the child-size plastic tunnel that ran around a square inside. It was meant to keep the children happy while their parents shopped.

"Yes."

"They never had those when I was growing up. I've always wanted to go through one of those."

His brows, so expressive, rose. "What for?"

"For the fun of it."

"There are other ways to have fun, Ms. Tynan."

She laughed, then began walking toward the next window, eager to see what the other merchants had done with their windows. "I mean so I could be with kids—kids who can talk and walk and explore the wonders of the world. Not babies," she said conversationally.

It took him a moment or so to catch up with her thoughts and answer them. "I thought all women liked babies."

"I don't know about all women. Just me, and I do. And I will know more about them when I have one of my own. But for now, I like the ones that can tell me what they need." She chewed her carrot stick, then reached for another one. "My goddaughter, Brenna, is three, and it's a wonderful age."

"I thought three was an awful age."

Crystal stopped and thought a moment. "No. I think those are the terrible twos."

"You mean they turn three, and the terrible twos are over? Candles, cakes and then the big change?" he asked.

Crystal slowed in midstep. Her eyes widened as she looked up at him in wonder. "You just made a joke."

He stopped and faced her, blocking out the current window dressing. "And?"

"I'm startled. That's all." She was shocked, but she wouldn't let him know how shocked she was.

"Why?"

"Well," she began, studying the faint crinkle lines around his beautiful blue eyes. If he ever fully smiled, her heart better watch out! "Until now, you've hardly done anything but frown at me since we met this morning."

"That's not true." But the light in his eyes told the story. He just realized she was right, and how stern he'd been with her.

"Yes, it is," she contested softly, gently, unwilling to begin another argument but not willing to agree for the sake of agreement, either. "And your smile is dynamite, as is the twinkle in your handsome blue eyes."

Blake gave a rueful sigh. "First you accuse me of being a grouch, act as if I'm anal retentive, and then you tell me I'm handsome. Are you always so direct?"

"I try to be," she said modestly, pleased that he could at least read her correctly. There might be hope for him yet, even though it'd be with another woman. "And don't forget honest."

He gave a laugh, delightful lines crinkling at the corners of his eyes again. His smile truly was dynamite, when he used it. Darn. Taking his arm, she turned him around and began walking again. "Well, in that case, Blake, you can continue with me on this quest of mine for a lesson in window dressing—as long as you occasionally smile."

"Another sexist remark, Ms. Tynan?" Blake asked dryly. "If a man said that, he'd be considered a pig."

"So be it, Blake," she said, laughter in her voice. "But there has to be some retribution for your sex's behavior over the past two thousand years. I'm just one woman doing my part to show you the way to change your outlook and ego stance."

"You flatter me. I feel so..."

"Feminine?" she interjected.

"No. Like a sex object."

"Lucky you," she said, patting his arm. "You never know when it's your lucky day."

His laughter was so delightfully sexy, Crystal had to stop and look at him again. The pride of making him laugh warmed her insides. Without thinking, she went on tiptoe and touched his lips, lightly brushing them with hers. "Thank you for such a delightful sound."

His laughter stopped and he sucked in his breath. "You're welcome," he finally managed to say. But he sounded strangled and the hold on her hand against his body tightened.

She liked that.

One of the women's lingerie store windows was having a chilly month, displaying seductive bras and panties in cream and white silks and rayons on mannequins also wearing winter hats. Large snowflakes on invisible strings hung from the ceiling and the floor was covered in tiny snowflakes.

Crystal stopped and stared, making mental notes of the techniques that the window dresser had used to emphasize the hot, sexy appeal of the undergarments in the snowstorm scene. She paid close attention to where thumbtacks were secured, what kind of paper was used to create the snowflakes and how the mannequins were positioned and the choices of lingerie on view from affordable to extravagant.

"Ms. Tynan?" Blake's voice was low but urgent.

"Mmm?" she asked, still staring at the details of the window.

"Can we leave this setting?"

"What?" She looked up at him. It took a minute to recognize a *definitely uncomfortable male.* "Oh," she said. "Let's go."

He didn't say anything, but the expression on his handsome face revealed his relief. Crystal chewed another carrot stick to hide her smile as they continued to stroll through the mall.

Blake stopped in front of a cafeteria, where the line was already out the door. "Can I interest you in something to eat?"

"Not today, but if you ask me tomorrow, I'll be

sure not to bring my lunch." She looked around. "I like cafeterias. They cater to my weird taste."

"Somehow, I knew that."

"Good, then we'll meet tomorrow for lunch?" she asked.

"Tomorrow," he confirmed, glancing at his watch.

If she hadn't known better, she'd have said he was reluctant to end their meeting until that telltale look at the time. He obviously had an appointment scheduled. That wasn't good for the digestion, but until she could teach him differently, it was his way.

"See you tomorrow," she promised with a smile. And with a wave, Crystal set off down the other side of the mall, still peering into windows and studying the various display techniques.

She felt Blake's eyes on her for a few moments, then she knew he'd disappeared.

He was an oddity. So handsome, yet he didn't seem to be quite aware of it himself. So uptight in his thoughts and actions, that he believed it was normal to be so shut off from others. So sophisticated in business, yet unable to study a window that had women's underwear. And he had one heck of a great body, but didn't eat carrot sticks....

Unusual to say the least.

Crystal knew she was a bit unconventional, but she wasn't that far out of the loop of normal! And she was told she had a great sense of humor—of course she was told that by friends who shared the same sense of sublime silliness.

Besides, she had as much of a right to be silly or

businesslike as much as she had a right to be herself. It took her a while to realize it, but she knew now that she could be anything she wanted to be without having to fit into someone else's idea of normal or conventional. In the past few years she'd noticed something startling: everyone's idea of normal was different.

Aunt Helen was right. You can't please everyone all the time, so please yourself first—as long as it doesn't hurt someone else.

Her watch told her that if she hurried, she'd have ten minutes to eat her lunch. Yogurt and two pieces of fresh fruit along with a bottle of water flavored with cranberry juice awaited her in the back room.

Surprisingly, her first day on the job at Aunt Helen's store was the most fun she'd had in a while. She couldn't wait to see how she felt tomorrow, when she had lunch with Blake Wright.

Crystal grinned. It was funny to call him Blake while he called her Ms. Tynan. But she refused to give up the right to call him by his first name. In every telephone conversation with her aunt over the past two years, Helen had referred to him as Blake. Crystal wasn't about to learn a new name for the man her aunt had spoken of. Part of her was hoping she'd come to know the same Blake as her aunt did. *That* Blake had a sense of humor and was a lot of fun, if her aunt was to be believed—and if the peek at him she'd just had was really real. In fact, Crystal was praying for him to be the same. The glimpses of the man she'd seen beneath his disapproving attitude was nice. Sweet. And very human.

It was that stiff attitude he occasionally wore that she wasn't too sure of being able to handle without giving him directions on where to take it. But then, if she could handle her boss, Tim, at the lodge, she could handle anything. Now *there* was a stiff. The difference was, she wasn't the least bit interested in seeing if there was another side to Tim. She had to admit, at least to herself, that she would love to see the other side of Blake.... If only for a little while.

BLAKE WATCHED Crystal walk away, his eyes straying from her small shoulders and tiny waist to her swaying hips. Her walk was free and sensuous and feminine. Her shoulders moved with a rhythm that was also feminine. But if he'd seen that walk on a male, he'd have called it cocky. On this woman, it was just damn sexy.

He gave himself a mental shake, and deliberately looked away. What the hell was on his mind that he would get so wrapped up in a woman's walk? Especially this woman?

She was his opposite and he was astute enough to know it. Although she was beautiful in a very unusual way, there was more that called to a male than her looks. It was the light behind her eyes. The promise of her constantly uptilted lips. The softness of her body in all the right places.

She was made for loving. Like it or not, he had to admit he was drawn to her physically. And that could never be if he wanted to keep his friendship with Helen. After all, he couldn't be friends with the aunt, whom he genuinely liked and admired, while making love to the niece until he tired of the kook. It wasn't right. Crystal wasn't right for him.

Too free-spirited.

Too casual.

Too...sexy.

Blake strode to the food court and ordered a roast beef sandwich, then took it back into his office to work through lunch.

But all through his meal, he was angry with himself for his body's intense reaction to Crystal's sexiness in the first place.

She was just exactly the wrong type for him.

BY THE TIME Crystal turned out the store lights for the night and twisted the key in the lock, she was excited. She had crammed her day with learning something new every hour, and it had paid off. Her creative juices were flowing like Niagara Falls.

Her aunt's business was good, with repeat customers making up at least sixty percent of the business. Her small knickknacks and floral decorations were beautiful, if a bit bland.

But Crystal would love to buy a few different, oddball items, mix them in with the bland stuff and dress up the store with unusual, one-of-a-kind decorator touches. Do some different stuff, as her friend, Ouida Vestal, used to say.

Still thinking of things she'd like to do, she drove

to her aunt's home. It was on the side of a hill with the desert stark and beautiful in one direction, and the beginning of a wide canyon filled with trees at the back door. Her aunt and uncle had been lucky enough to find a piece of property that had the best of both worlds and had made the most of it. Her aunt owned enough of the land to block out someone's building and ruining her view.

When Crystal walked into the house, she took a deep breath. The chill outside air counterpointed the scents wafting from the kitchen. Pot roast, fresh bread and some kind of pie.

"I'm home!" she called, taking off her sweater and hanging it in the hallway. "And you're supposed to be resting!"

"I'm glad you're home and I am resting!" her aunt called back.

Crystal walked into the large den area and found her mother's twin sitting in a deep-yellow upholstered chair with her feet on the matching ottoman. Her arm was in a cast and swathed in a beautiful silk scarf instead of the usual, hospital-issued, cotton sling. It was coordinated with her matching maroon silk pajamas. She was watching the fireplace and listening to the television.

"How was the shop?" she asked, lifting her head for her niece's kiss. Her hennaed hair was cut short in the back but long on top, with soft curls going in every direction. Aunt Helen was a good-looking woman. Her eyes were much like Crystal's, a rich deep brown, but radiated the wisdom and maturity of her fifty years.

"It was the most fun I've had with my clothes on." Crystal got a slap on the bottom for that wild remark.

Instead of commenting on the hit, she took the matching chair, propped up her feet and leaned back, loving the luxury of doing nothing. "It's a great little store. I brought the receipts home with me so you can show me what to deposit and how to call in the charges, then enter them into Hugo, over there." She aimed her chin toward the computer hidden in the armoire section of the wall unit. "Were you so afraid of my cooking you had to put yourself through hours in the kitchen?"

"Not at all," Aunt Helen said calmly. "Michael brought over a pie, Kenneth and his daughter made a pot roast with potatoes and carrots, and Mab, next door, just made homemade rolls." She grinned. "So we have dinner compliments of my friends."

"How nice. Better still, what nice friends." Crystal meant it. Her aunt seemed to draw people to her like moths to a flame. It was no wonder, she had warmth and a sense of fun that was contagious.

"I'm lucky, and in more than one way, darling. Most of the men my age are looking for a wife, and they're ready to do whatever it takes to have one so they're not alone."

"And you're willing to help them in this?"

"Not at all. I don't have time," her aunt replied calmly.

"No? Come on," Crystal said, disbelieving.

Her aunt sighed dramatically. "So many men, so little time."

"I can't believe you really said that."

Aunt Helen chuckled. "Don't worry. It's not true. I'm a widow and at an age when most single men are getting panicked because they don't have someone to take care of them in their old age. They're beating the bushes at the same time they're showing eligible women how self-sufficient they are."

"And are you?" Crystal said, finally stirring enough to realize her aunt probably needed a little something to drink. "Eligible, I mean."

"Never. Not on a bet." The older woman laughed. "I'm not about to ruin a good thing by allowing someone to think of me as a wife instead of a marvelous, seductive woman to be sought and captured...almost."

Crystal stretched and sat up. It had been a long day. "Can I get you a glass of ice water?"

"No, thank you. I already drank enough to make a camel jealous." She watched her niece walk into the kitchen. "Check the pot roast would you?"

Crystal did, then came out with two glasses of white Chablis. "Dinner will be ready whenever you are, Aunt Helen." She handed her aunt one of the glasses.

"So, tell me about your day," Helen asked eagerly as she took a sip of the cooled wine. "Did you meet Blake yet?"

"I certainly did. He's as handsome as you said he

was, but with very little humor and even less of an easy manner. In fact, he was the most uptight man I've ever met."

"Blake?" Her aunt sounded confused.

That obviously wasn't strong enough to make an impression on her aunt. Crystal decided she had to emphasize the fact that she felt cheated by his attitude. "Even the millionaires I work with aren't that uptight."

Helen's eyes widened in disbelief. "Blake?" she repeated.

"Blake," Crystal reaffirmed. "I spent half an hour with him this morning, then we walked around the mall a little."

"Walked around the mall?" Now Aunt Helen sounded downright disbelieving.

Crystal nodded then continued. "In all that time, he smiled twice—well maybe three times. But that was it. The rest of the time he looked at me as if I were a two-day-old fish."

"I'm so surprised," Helen stated. "He's always been so warm and fun with me. Although we've never walked around the mall, we've been friends ever since we first met."

"Maybe he's interested in you," Crystal suggested. The words didn't taste any better on her tongue than the thought had.

"If he was," Helen stated, "it's the best kept secret in the mall. Even I don't know about it. But then, there's too much of an age difference between us."

"Men and women have had eighteen-year age differences before, and overcame it."

"Yes, but not women and men. This is a different difference, and I'm not willing to have a relationship with someone that young any more than I'm willing to have one with someone that much older than I am."

Crystal giggled.

"Now stop ignoring the topic of conversation and tell me what else happened with Blake."

"Not much." Crystal gave a shrug and glanced out the back window at the sharp edge of forest. "All he did was give me disapproving looks and tell me what he thought was wrong with my way of thinking."

"Now, I wonder why I don't believe that." Her aunt didn't meet her eyes. Instead, she rearranged her scarf. "You spent a long time with the man. Longer than anyone else he doesn't know."

"Really?" she asked, trying to ignore the flash of delight her aunt's words delivered. "I didn't notice. It's probably because of his friendship with you."

"Of course," Helen stated dryly. "Why didn't I think of that? You're my niece so he's sworn to spend an hour with you because he is worried about me. It's his way of sending greetings instead of visits or dinner."

"Well, it really doesn't matter," Crystal stated airily as she stood and walked toward the kitchen. "He's just a friend of yours who, in his own stiff way, tried to be friendly to me for the day. It's over and now I'll get us dinner."

"Methinks, my niece, that you doth protest too much," Helen said, a lilt in her tone.

"Methinks, my aunt, that you have a problem perceiving relationship problems." She refused to mention she was having lunch with Blake tomorrow. It was a secret she wanted to keep to herself for a little while longer.

They ate while watching the news, each one easy with the other's presence. It was relaxing and nice, reminding Crystal of her teenage years when her own mother had died and Helen had become her surrogate mom. It had been a rough time, but Aunt Helen had made it bearable.

But dancing in the back of Crystal's mind were some of the windows she'd seen in the mall. She wanted to try her hand at something different than the ordinary and average. She wasn't sure how, yet. But if she studied the problem, it would come to her.

Solutions always did.

Half an hour after the news, she kissed her aunt good-night. "I'll see you in the morning, dear. If you need me, call and I'll hear you."

"I'll be fine, Crystal. I broke my arm, not my head. And I feel frustrated enough not being able to the do what I want," the older woman groused. "Just give me another week or two, and I'll find my stride again."

"I'll give you six weeks, Aunt. No less," she promised, leaning over and giving her a kiss on the cheek. "See you tomorrow."

But after Crystal was in her bedroom at the end of the hall for fifteen minutes, she found herself too keyed up to be able to sleep. No matter what, her thoughts wound back to Blake and their talk. She relived everything he said and did. Every movement he made. Every emotion that he brought out in her. And she became more awake by the minute.

He was so frustrating. Was there a wild, devil-may-care bone in his body? Did he ever run naked through his apartment? What about belly laughs that massaged his every organ?

Forcing herself to focus on something else, she lit one of the scented candles she'd brought with her from Santa Fe and sat cross-legged in the center of her bed. With her hands palms up and open to all kinds of possibilities, she took several deep breaths to cleanse her body of all the pent-up carbon monoxide she'd cultivated all day. After a few minutes, she did her transcendental meditation. If it was good enough for half the doctors in the world to proclaim it as calming medication for the heart, then it was good enough for her to quickly erase the provocative image of a more free, spontaneous, Blake Wright running through a field of mountain flowers in joyous abandon—naked.

She hoped.

3

"SO FAR, your floral designs with the wild color combinations have sold like hotcakes!" Standing at the cash register, Linda sounded just a little shocked by that fact as she watched a woman holding one of Crystal's floral arrangements walk out of the store.

Crystal, standing at the work counter, laughed. "It's the price, Linda. My creations don't sell for as much as Aunt Helen's or yours because they're not as elaborate."

"Oh, I'm sure, and the colors aren't found in the usual *Entrée* type of arrangements." She sounded so puzzled that Crystal almost felt sorry for her.

"I know, but you see, customers get to walk out of here with an original from a very exclusive shop and feel as if they got a bargain."

Linda's face lit up. "Of course. They get the *Entrée* name without paying the full *Entrée* price or getting the *Entrée* colors." Her words finally sunk into her own thoughts and her eyes widened. "Oh! I didn't mean that your efforts weren't good! I mean, they must be or they wouldn't have sold at all and they'd still be sitting on the shelf and not being sold...."

Crystal gave her new friend a hug. "Don't worry. I understand what you're trying to say and I appreciate it. But I know they're not the same as what the store usually stocks."

Then yet another customer came up to the counter with one of Crystal's creations and set it down. Without saying a word, she pulled out her Visa card and offered it in payment.

"The yellow, blue and cream," Linda said, as amazed as she'd been earlier.

It took everything Crystal had to make sure she didn't laugh aloud. "That will be thirty-six dollars," she said as she ran the card through the machine.

Within seconds she had a funny feeling. A very distinct and definite funny feeling.

Blake was close by.

She handed the woman a pen while her gaze searched the front door area. But she'd waited too late to spot him there. He was already inside the shop and standing to the right of the register area, studying one of her creations with a quizzical look on his somber handsome face. Obviously, he didn't understand the attraction, either.

Crystal would have bet that the colors and design were just a little too wild for Blake to take a liking to. It wasn't his taste at all. Just like its creator.

Just then, he looked up and locked eyes with her. He stared at her as deeply as he had examined the arrangement. Just for a change of pace—and to shock him a little by proving she could do it if she wanted to—Crystal had worn makeup at full war-paint level and had wrapped her hair to the top back of her head, securing it with an Oriental hair pin. It ached to be let loose and fall and tumble about her shoulders. Small, golden tendrils curled around her hairline, emphasizing her features. Then she topped it off with a short-skirted navy suit with a bright-red blouse. And high—very high—heels.

It was an occasion. She donned this outfit maybe once a year and reveled in the double takes she got from people who knew her. Until Blake said something about it, she wasn't going to comment, either. But his reaction was worth a thousand words. She just wanted to prove she could look the executive when she wanted to. He'd probably never see it again.

"Are you here to identify me in a lineup, or to take me to lunch?" she asked casually while separating the paper receipts. She turned back to her customer before he could answer. "Thank you for your business, and if we can help you customize an arrangement, please let us know. We'll be glad to make one with your personal colors."

"Thank you," the woman said delightedly. "I'll keep that in mind."

"So, you remembered we were having lunch today?" he asked, after the customer had left the store.

"Of course. I was just waiting for you to tell me where to meet you." She grinned. "You could have saved yourself the trip and called with the info. I could have met you."

His gaze wandered down her body, straying here and there and causing heat to rise in her like sap in spring. It was supposed to be the other way around.

She was supposed to light *his* fire. But he never cracked a smile at her choice of wardrobe. "I always pick up my dates."

"In that case, Blake, I'm ready." Ignoring his formality, she moved over to his side, took his arm and gave a short wave to Linda, who was watching as if there was nothing else going on in the world.

"Where are we going?" Crystal said as they passed through the store and into the mall area.

He tightened his arm at his side as if to keep and capture her hand. "To my office. Do you mind?"

Crystal stopped and, unwilling to let her go, Blake stopped with her, waiting for her to speak.

"Are you attempting to ravish my body during lunch without permission?" she asked, cautiously.

A light flared in his deep-blue eyes. "No. I'd never do that."

Darn. He was still in control and still building tension between them. Blake was some kinda guy. "Are your intentions honorable?"

His sculpted mouth twitched. "Of course."

She laughed softly. "Liar."

"That's not true. If I say it, I mean it." He finally let a small smile through. "Although I can only guarantee now, Ms. Tynan. I can't guarantee later."

An almost joke. He was warming up, and warming up her heart, too. She tugged on his arm. "Let's go, then. You can't do anything without getting between me and my food. I won't stand for it."

"Now I know where your priorities lie," he said,

his steady gait once more leading her toward his office.

She kept pace by taking two rickety steps to every one he took. But she wasn't going to admit how hard it was for her to walk on stilts. Instead, she continued to trip along. "You seem like the kind of guy who always knew where you stood. Since the age of two, anyway."

"What makes you say that?" he asked, obviously surprised at her observation.

"Because you're so controlled. So..." she began.

"Rigid?" His husky voice sounded as dry as dust.

This wasn't the time to lie. After all, she didn't know him well enough to lie, yet. For something like that, you had to have a history and want to save someone's feelings. "So you know."

"If I didn't know before, I've got that feeling now."

"From me?" she asked.

He held open the office glass door. Marilyn wasn't at her desk. *"Especially* from you." He took her arm and led her firmly past his office into the conference room.

"I'm so sorry if I..." Crystal stopped. The walnut conference table had a thick, white tablecloth draped over one end. The table was set formally, right down to crystal water glasses. "Oh, my," she breathed.

She had expected cafeteria food on a tray or from a metal basket lined with paper. Or maybe sandwiches in clear, plastic sleeves. But this...well, this was far more than she'd imagined. The privacy, good linens, formal setting—all, made it so very special.

Plain white containers covered in shiny metal sat in front of the place settings. Crystal lifted a cover and sniffed. Then lifted another cover and sniffed again before looking over her shoulder at the man who watched her so intently. It smelled heavenly. "Thai?"

"Vietnamese."

Her eyes lit up. "Um, spicy."

"Yes." He grinned. "I figured it fit you." His slow grin was catching, to say nothing about sexy as all-get-out.

She gave a short curtsy, proud of herself for not letting her stiletto heels tip her over. "Thank you."

Blake pulled out a side chair and offered her the seat. Feeling like the princess in a fairy tale, Crystal took it. Blake sat at the end of the table and reached for his napkin. Crystal followed suit, a little slower than Blake. She was so conscious of his every move—until the tantalizing scent of well-prepared food wafted her way again and reminded her stomach just how hungry she was.

Without hesitating any longer, she helped herself to sampling the containers on the table. "Is this from one of the mall restaurants?" she asked, taking a double helping of the freshly steamed vegetables.

"No, it's from a restaurant downtown." Blake helped himself from a far container, then passed it to her. "Have you eaten Vietnamese before?"

"Yes, and I love it." Crystal took a bite and rolled

her eyes, drawing another smile from Blake. Good. Getting a good reaction from him was more satisfying than a full stomach.

They talked about foods and restaurant experiences they treasured. Crystal watched his mouth move, his changing expressions flow across his face and enjoyed his smile and twinkling blue eyes as he relaxed. Even if he was a little uptight, the man was far more fascinating than anything he could state about food. Not that she didn't like the topic.

"This is my second favorite topic of conversation," she announced, then watched his eyes light up again.

"Can I ask?"

"No." Her smile softened the negative reply. Why would he want to talk about massage therapy right now?

Blake reached for a small thermal coffee pot and poured them both some. She indulged him in it. She hadn't said no, and certainly hadn't mentioned in their conversations that she only drank green tea. Besides, a couple of sips of coffee wouldn't hurt.

"Do you always wear suits?" she asked, noting his sophisticated blue suit.

"Most of the time. Especially when I'm at work."

"Why not more casual?"

"You have something against suits?" Those thick brows rose in challenge.

But she wasn't stopping now. "They're very formal. Don't you find they put the average mall customer off?"

"I don't run into the average mall customer very often, Crystal," he reminded her in a voice that said he was teaching someone the rudiments about his job. "I deal with executives across the country who need space for stores, or specialty-shop owners who can afford long leases. I check them out financially and make the best deal for the mall corporation, whom I represent."

"Then who takes care of any complaints from customers or security?"

"My secretary handles customers, along with a part-time young man who acts as an assistant. And Jet, a retired policeman is head of security and the guards."

"Oh." It wasn't anything like she imagined. Somehow, she'd thought of him as working on a slightly smaller scale. "So you work with the major department stores as well as the small stores like *Entrée*?"

"Right."

He was one man against the many. "You must get tired of the pressure by the end of the day."

"Especially physically." He smiled, dodging her question. "I get tired of standing on my feet on concrete when I'm negotiating space. Then sooner or later, I get a backache from the tension."

"I don't doubt it."

"In fact," he said, stretching out his legs and heaving a sigh. "That's what I've been doing for the past three days."

"And are the people you're dealing with going to rent space?"

"Don't know yet. I've got another two or three weeks, maybe months to negotiate with them. They're a major department store that the Chamber of Commerce wants to see build in the city. So do I, but not for the same reasons."

She didn't think about what she was about to do. She just did it. Crystal pushed her chair back and reached between them, wrapping her palm around his ankle and pulled it up to her lap.

"What are you doing?" he asked, startled.

"I won't hurt you. Just relax," she commanded. "I'm rubbing your foot. It's what I do for a living, remember?"

She untied his wing tip's shoelaces and slipped off his shoe, ignoring his tugging against her. "Wing tips? I thought they went out with my grandfather."

He pulled his foot away again, but she resisted. "Crystal..." he began.

He called her Crystal. That made her feel so much better. The formality was finally over, and all it had taken was exposing his foot. Patting the sole, she reassured him. "Can't you take a gift? I usually charge people to do this—and they line up for the opportunity."

Blake hesitated only seconds more before resigning himself to her touch. She began rubbing the bottom pads of his well-clad toes, one by one.

"I'm not sure this is done on a first date." Blake eventually sighed, leaning back and completely giving in to her touch.

"Really?" She rotated the ball of his foot, then his ankle. "Are you saying this is a real first date?"

"Mmm. What did you think? That I ask all store managers to lunch?"

"No, I thought you were doing this because of my aunt," she said. All her concentration was on his foot. He had a good, strong foot with a high arch. An excellent sign of a healthy body. She made a fist and rubbed the arch to heel, then back again.

Blake groaned in delight. The deep, rough sound was erotic, sending chills down her spine. He cleared his throat. "This isn't very romantic, Crystal."

She rubbed her knuckles along the side of his foot. "Really? What do you think is romantic? Sex?"

He looked startled, his blue eyes widening. "Are you always so blunt?"

She wouldn't tell him that her curiosity wouldn't settle for less. "Would you rather I act coy and charming and not let you know what I'm thinking or how I'm feeling?" She rubbed the ball of each toe, especially the big one, to stimulate his brain.

He gave a small satisfied grunt as she hit the spot that marked his inhibitions. He was most tense there. Good. He could stand loosening up a little. "Does it have to be one way or the other? Isn't there a happy medium?"

"There is, but most people don't recognize it when they see it." She rubbed his toes again, taking slow care to work each underside pad for his spine. "For instance, I never said a word about your shoes before now. Nor did I mention sex. I kept it to myself and got no credit for doing so, until now."

"Thank you," he said.

She gave a smile that told him she wasn't giving up on the discussion. "You mentioned romance and I wanted to know your opinion. Is sex the same as romance to you?"

Giving a quick glance through her lashes, she found him carefully studying her. If she hadn't looked, she never would have known that his skin seemed to have tanned and flushed highlights. He was blushing.

Interesting.

"Sex is a part of romance." It sounded more like a strangled confession than a conversation. He obviously didn't talk about it much. If ever.

Crystal's fingers stroked the back of the heel, then worked up to the ankle bone, rubbing and stimulating that part of his foot which, according to reflexology, was connected to his sexual organs. Her fingers massaged softly yet firmly. She knew what she was doing, but he didn't.

His flush increased.

It wasn't fair. She shouldn't be stimulating him this way. After all, she wasn't willing to do anything about the sexual feelings she was creating.

"Let me have your other foot," she said, patting the top of his foot to let him know she was through.

"Hmmm?" he asked absently, observing his foot as if it belonged to someone else.

She lowered his foot to the floor. "Your other foot?"

Blake sat up straight. "Oh, no, that's not necessary," he said briskly.

"You'd better take advantage of me now, Blake. I'm here and I'm willing, so give me your other foot and let me complete the job." Crystal leaned forward to reach for his other foot, but stopped in midreach.

Blake stared back, his eyes delving into her in a way that washed chill bumps down her spine. Thoughts better left unsaid passed between them. Vivid, heated images flashed through her mind, and all of them had to do with making love with the man in front of her.

Keeping his eyes locked with hers, very slowly, Blake leaned forward. He came closer and closer to Crystal. Without a doubt, she knew what was going to happen. It was written in his eyes and flooded through her in the form of want. Want to taste. Want to touch. Every warning bell in her went off loudly. This man wasn't for her. He wasn't wealthy, he wasn't free and easy. He wasn't funny or people-oriented. No. Not at all.

Yet, while thinking all this so clearly, she leaned even closer, meeting him halfway across the space that divided them. His warm breath flowed across her face like a caress. His sculpted mouth was so close to her own that she could touch him with her lips to sip just a little taste of him. That ought to soothe her appetite.

Just one taste...

Blake's mouth pulled back, just inches from hers. "I'm going to kiss you," he said, his voice rough and deep, running like a shivering-cold river through her.

"I wish you would."

He was no longer Mr. Nice Guy. "Come here," he ordered.

And she did.

When his mouth touched hers, Crystal's breath caught in her throat. A wonderful zing slipped down her spine, then pulsated through the rest of her. He brushed her lips, then brushed again before capturing hers, holding her captive with the touch of his mouth alone.

Mouth clung to mouth, his daring hers to remain passive and to ignore the intense chemistry that pulsed between them. She felt warm and bubbly and smooth and sweet and sexy, melting and melding with him. So many more emotions flowed through her—most she could not even begin to analyze. She couldn't; her mind wasn't working properly. It was engaging emotions without thought....

Blake's hand touched the side of her face, his fingers burying themselves in her thick strands of hair, holding her even closer. Crystal knew she wanted so much more of him than was possible. Right now.

Again, she ignored the clanging sound of warning bells. With both hands, she reached up to hold his head close while her tongue darted out to explore his. "More," she finally whispered. "I want more."

The moan that echoed from deep in his chest was her answer.

Before she could take action, he wrapped his arms around her waist and tugged her into the firm haven of his lap. He settled her within the confines of his legs.

She went willingly, circling her arms around his neck and holding on as if he were the lifeline in a turbulent sea.

Blake took command, teaching her quickly that she only thought she had initiated his interest. His lust. His own special brand of sexiness. His tongue led her in a sensuous dance that told her who was boss and why. The alpha male, the lone leader of the pack.

But she couldn't let him think that she was giving in. After all, she was female and also in charge. With hands that shook, she ran her fingers inside his jacket, lacing them across his chest, teasing his nipples through his lightly starched shirt as much as he teased her with his tongue and hands that circled and touched everywhere but on her heavy breasts.

Heaven. Heaven was the image of Blake lying her on the conference table and...

"Boss?" a female voice called.

Although Crystal heard the voice, it didn't register right away.

Blake pulled his mouth from hers and dragged in a harsh breath. His heart pumped heavily beneath her hand. "I'll be right there, Marilyn. Give me a minute, will you?"

"Right," she said. "You've got an appointment in half an hour."

It finally registered. Blake's secretary had almost walked into the room and caught them in a clinch that had far more to do with sex than sweetness.

She rested her forehead against his shoulder for a moment as she caught her breath. "You miscalculated," she murmured, afraid to raise her voice for fear it would crack with emotion.

"How?"

Crystal gathered her emotions together and tucked them away, to be diagnosed later. Right now she had to get out of here with dignity intact. "You should have kissed me earlier."

She stood and smoothed her skirt back down, pretending she was concerned with wrinkles when she couldn't even see them. Her eyes refused to focus.

"I should have," he replied, softly.

"My curiosity would have been appeased and we'd be back at work right about now." She dodged his gaze by looking at her watch. It was past her time to be back at the store. "Now we're both late."

"I should have kissed you the moment we walked in here," he repeated. "Then we could have had more time to play around." This time his tone was grim. There wasn't a shred of humor in his voice.

Her hand arrested his movement as he turned. "Hey, you," she teased softly. "Lighten up."

"I *am* lightened up."

His frown made lines directly over the bridge of his nose. "Good grief, I'd hate to see you in a mean mood." She turned and began closing the lids to the containers.

"Don't do that. The restaurant people will arrive in half an hour to pick it all up."

"Really? You're not taking the leftovers home?" That behavior didn't fit. Such a cautious man wouldn't throw money away.

He looked a little sheepish. "Yes."

She relaxed, feeling a little more secure about reading him correctly. She wasn't completely lost. "Then you'll need these containers closed before the food goes bad."

"Thank you," he said. His voice was still stiff and distant. "And I'm sorry if I took, uh, liberties. I shouldn't have."

"You are? Did you?" She reached for her purse, but didn't move away from the spot where she stood. They might as well get this over with now, or they'd never be able to look each other in the eye again. She forced herself to look at him. "I thought it was something mutual that happened. I didn't know I was blindly following and you were masterfully leading."

Blake's stern look hadn't gone away. "I'm responsible for how far we went, Crystal. And I wouldn't hurt you or Helen for the world."

"Ah, my aunt." Disappointment bubbled up inside. He wasn't afraid of offending her, but her aunt. Great. "Well, I'm sure she thanks you for your concern, but she's not in the room right now. I am."

"Dammit, I'm apologizing to you!"

"And I'll accept as long as it's a formality. I'll also let you know when there's something you need to apologize to me for." She turned away. "Thanks for the lunch, Blake. It was well worth the time, if not the apology."

She opened the door before he spoke. "Thank you, Ms. Tynan. I enjoyed it without apology."

Turning, she stared over her shoulder at him. Was that a small but not insignificant smile dancing around his sexy lips? Deliberately leaving the door opened, she walked back and stood in front of him, staring up at his mouth.

Blake stared back down, the smile slowly receding to his usual frown.

"That's what I thought," she said. "A smile actually flirted with your lips." Determined to ease the tension between them, she brushed a slow, light kiss across his mouth. "Thanks for the view. It was great."

Without waiting for his reply, she walked out of the room. There might have been a sexier little twitch to her hips, but if there was, it was just bravado. "Hi, Marilyn. Great lunch," she said as she passed his secretary's desk.

Marilyn looked up, surprised. "You're welcome," she answered seconds before Crystal was out the door and down the hallway.

But it wasn't until Crystal got back to the shop and into the bathroom that she realized all that makeup she'd worn was gone. She looked like someone who'd been pulled through a knothole during a storm.

She could have put a sign on her back that said Heavy Kissing Within Last Half Hour and it would answer just as many questions as the ones she saw in passersby's eyes.

She scrubbed her face clean and began the makeup process again, this time with very little makeup and no base. Taking her hair down from its Gibson knot, she twisted it tightly and slipped a large Oriental pin through it again, then straightened her suit and walked out as if nothing had happened.

Which of course, it hadn't. Kissing wasn't against the law, just an unwise action with a man she wasn't committed to. This was wrong for her, and she didn't have an excuse.

Crystal held her future needs in the forefront of her mind for the rest of the day. She visited shops, talked to salespeople and learned more about the business of retail sales. Along the way, she made some new friends, people with whom she'd enjoy socializing with....

So there, Blake Wright!

4

CRYSTAL HAD WORKED at the store five days before finally broaching her aunt on the topic of window dressing.

"Do you mind if I do something different with the windows?" she asked while eating oatmeal for dinner. It was almost eleven o'clock at night and she wasn't up to eating anything more complicated.

"Like what?" Aunt Helen asked, not letting her eyes leave the TV screen in case she missed one second of David Letterman's antics.

"I don't know yet."

A commercial came on and her aunt turned in her direction. "I have a man who comes by once a month to change the window display. He has a hundred more props than I have. Besides, Bart loves doing it and I find it boring."

"When does he come again?"

"Next Tuesday. His number is in the Rolodex file at work. Designer's Creations is the name of the company. He'll do whatever you have in mind, or he'll do what *he* has in mind. But, if it's something you want, you've got to let him know in advance, so he knows what to bring."

"Maybe I'll work with him on this, since you don't mind."

"Not at all." The commercials were over and Helen turned back to the screen. "I'd rather make arrangements and decorate the shop than play with that big window."

"I just thought that it'd be a great experience to try. Something new to learn." And fun enough to keep her mind occupied with something other than Blake.

"That's fine, honey. Whatever you want to try as long as it's within the guidelines of mall regulations."

Crystal looked up from sketches she'd made earlier that evening. "Regulations?"

"Yes. Blake can tell you more about them, but the mall has regulations about what you can put in the window and how it's displayed. It's like deed restrictions in a housing area."

"I see." There went a few of her more—uh, slightly eccentric ideas. She tapped the spoon against her empty bowl as she thought of the others. They might be okay....

The Letterman show was winding down and Helen stood and stretched her one good arm. "I forgot to tell you, I have a file in my office here that I keep all the papers for doing my own windows. It shows how to do the cost estimates and ideas I found elsewhere, along with a few other tips. If you want to look through it, it's in the second file drawer from the top. Under Window Dressings."

"Thanks!" Crystal got up and retrieved the folder. Her aunt came in just as she sat down at the office desk and opened it.

"Good night, dear." Her aunt kissed the top of her head, then patted Crystal's shoulder. "I love you."

"I love you, too. See you in the morning." Crystal watched her walk out, then returned her attention to the file.

She felt like a kid with a new toy....

THE FOLLOWING MORNING, Crystal felt like an old rag doll. Lack of sleep affected her that way. When she got involved in something new, she focused all her attention on it. She'd stayed up until just before 3:00 a.m. But she was determined to plunge ahead with her ideas. She took the fabric store manager, Darlene, to coffee that morning.

Once they were seated in the booth, Crystal told her the reason for the meeting. "If you ever want to use our live or silk flowers for a display inside the store, I'd be happy to work with you on that. In return, I'm plying you with dry cookies and coffee so that you'll let me have six yards of fabric for my window display."

Darlene gave a laugh. She was about Crystal's age, and apparently knew everything there was to know about cloth and material, and could even sew. And sew very well, from the looks of the sophisticated but casual outfit she wore.

"Well, I've never done that sort of thing before," she said, sipping her coffee. "But I don't see a problem with it. Can I show you the remnants and let you go through them or do you have some particular piece of material or color in mind?"

Crystal relaxed. The art of bartering was in place. "I have some ideas, but I'll start looking wherever you want me to. If that doesn't work, we'll look elsewhere. How does that sound?"

"Sounds good to me. Can we work on this after Monday? I have my district manager coming in this weekend and I've got oodles of records to check before he gets there."

"No problem. I'll aim my search for Monday," she said, pulling out her small appointment book from her purse and writing in a space. "I'll drop by then."

"Perfect."

"I'd say the same thing," a deep male voice interrupted, and Crystal's nerves recognized the voice instantly.

Darlene's eyes widened. "Mr. Wright. What a nice surprise."

"Hi, Blake." Crystal tried to be light and breezy. Thank goodness she had that part of her act down pat, or she'd do what Darlene was doing—stare. "Darlene and I were sharing trade secrets and stale six o'clock coffee at eleven," Crystal said, looking up into those vivid-blue eyes. His sandy-brown hair ached for fingers—hers—to run through it. Just like yesterday... Crystal swallowed hard.

"Are you here for the same thing?" Darlene asked.

"Yes, and I'd love some." He waved to the waiter and indicated a round of coffee for all of them. Then he squeezed into the booth next to Crystal. Suddenly a smile grew as he glanced at Darlene. "How are you, Darlene?"

"I'm fine, thank you." Darlene kept staring at him as if he were from another planet—or a Chippendale dancer. "How's tricks? Well, I didn't mean how's tricks, I meant how's business?" Her face turned beet-red.

"I'm familiar with the expression, Darlene. I knew what you meant, and thanks for asking. I'm fine," he said. Still smiling.

Damn him, couldn't he do that with her on occasion? All she ever got were his looks of disapproval, shock or surprise. Well, that was almost true. Yesterday at lunch was the exception. In fact, after the shock of seeing her in that power suit yesterday, he had smiled almost all through lunch. She hated to admit that Blake's head could be turned and his thoughts rearranged by a set of high heels and not-too-bad legs, but in that respect, all men were alike. On the other hand, it proved he was just a man. A double-edged sword.

Fresh coffee was brought to them as Blake turned to Crystal. "How has your Wednesday been so far?"

Nothing could beat yesterday, but she wasn't about to tell him that. "Just peachy."

"And do you have a full calendar for the weekend yet?"

"Full, as in…?" Crystal asked. She crossed her legs hoping he was going to ask what she thought he was going to ask.

He did.

"Do you have room for a party Saturday night?"

She smiled, delight warming her through and through. "Why Blake Wright, you rascal you. You do parties? I'm amazed."

The glimmer in his intense blue eyes proved he would have said more if Darlene hadn't been a witness, but his somber expression never changed. "Some friends are getting together, and I thought you'd enjoy getting out."

Laughter bubbled up inside, lighting up her eyes. "I'm saying yes before you change your mind and we both agree I'm not your type. I'd love to go to the party with you. Or the movies. Or perhaps, another lunch? With you paying, of course." A barely concealed smile was held in check. Almost. It was too much fun to confront him. She didn't have the time to be embarrassed over the day before.

"Right now, we're talking about the party."

Watching him feel a little uncomfortable right now made up for her feeling the same way earlier when she'd wondered if she would run into him and if so, how she would act. And here, by sitting with her, he'd made it all so much easier. She smiled. "I'm just a stranger passin' through, sir, and I'd love your company."

"I take it the answer is yes," Blake stated dryly, but his smile was even more wide than hers.

"Yes."

He stood. "Good, now that that's settled, I'll get on with my business." He held out his hand to Darlene, who placed hers in his. "It was good seeing you, Darlene. Hope we meet again, soon."

"Thanks," she said shyly.

"The waiter is giving us the high sign." Crystal didn't mind if Blake took her hint and paid their coffee bill.

The knowing twinkle in his eyes was aimed directly at her. "It's my pleasure to pay this time, Ms. Tynan."

She watched him as he peeled off a few bills and gave them to the waiter, then turned down the aisle that led back to the mall. She squashed the feeling of missing him instantly. That wouldn't do.

"You must know him pretty well," Darlene commented as Crystal watched him walk away.

Crystal turned back to her new friend. "I met him Monday. Why?"

Darlene's voice was filled with admiration. "Most of the mall's store managers are a little intimidated by him. But not you. You just made him pay for our coffee."

"He can afford to pay for coffee if he's going to drink with us and then ask for a favor."

"A date," Darlene corrected, chuckling.

"Well," Crystal corrected with a smile. "He's asking *me*, so they're both the same thing."

Darlene lost it. The sound of laughter bubbled through the luncheonette and Crystal's voice joined her.

"I love it," Darlene gurgled. "I think the intimidating Mr. Wright might have met his match."

"He has," Crystal confirmed. "But he just doesn't know it yet. By the time he realizes that little fact, I'll be long gone."

"When is that?"

"The day after Valentine's Day."

"I'm gonna miss you, Crystal. At least when I return. I'm getting married on Valentine's Day. Then I've got a week-long honeymoon in Banff, Canada."

That magic word—marriage. "Congratulations! To whom and why?"

"His name is Danny, and I love him," Darlene said easily, her smile practically a swoon. "He's not what I was looking for in looks, but he was what I was looking for in spirit."

"How did you know?"

Darlene shrugged, floundering for the right words. "I didn't know right away. But Danny did, and wouldn't let me ignore him. When he finally got me to pay attention, I felt it, too. Full-blown love hit me over the head, stunning me. It's been four years since we started dating, and I still feel the same way, only better." She smiled dreamily. "I want to feel this way for the next hundred years."

"Wow," Crystal whispered, awed by the look on her new friend's face. She wanted love. She wished for love. She craved to have it returned in kind. But she was a realist. Those emotions might not be for everyone. She'd never felt more than a twinge in all her life. But to have Darlene experience love after four years of being together with her guy and still have that feeling be so strong—well, that was wonderfully reassuring.

"Some day I want that, too," Crystal admitted. "But he has to be pretty special for marriage."

"Don't they all?" Darlene finished off her coffee. "Otherwise, why bother sharing your time and energy and deepest thoughts with someone who's not special?"

Crystal pushed away her empty cup. "I like the way you think, Darlene. How about lunch tomorrow? My treat." She stood and reached for her big knit bag.

Darlene scooted out of the bench. "Wonderful. I'm saving every penny I've got for the house, so your treat sounds great."

Once they separated, Crystal headed down the long wide corridor toward her aunt's store. On the way, she saw a music store and dashed in. "May I speak to the manager, please?" she asked, taking one more step into the area of window decorating. It was fun....

BLAKE WENT through the contract for a small store to rent space in the mall. It had been an easy go-round. The new client had used the mall's recommendations for a reasonably priced crew to build out the space the way the new store owners had envisioned. They were due to sign the contract this afternoon right after lunch.

It was an hour since he'd run into Crystal in the drugstore luncheonette. And she'd been in the back of his mind ever since. He couldn't believe his luck when he'd looked up and seen her. She had been in animated conversation with another woman he hadn't recognized. It hadn't mattered. His eyes had refused to budge from her.

Unlike most of the subdued, more formal women in his life, Crystal was so animated. Although not typically attractive, she'd create a stir anywhere. She had beauty and brains combined with a presence that made others notice her immediately. He couldn't keep his eyes off her. Her hands had gracefully danced in the air as she had spoken so energetically to her friend. The beginnings of a brilliant smile had teased the uptilted corners of her mouth. And her warm brown eyes, wide and excited, were man magnets. He'd guess that any man worth his salt would be drawn to her.

And he was jealous of any man who got near her.

That emotion was really stupid. That wasn't like him at all. He suspected that it was a passing fancy, but at least now he knew the meaning of that feeling. If ever someone mentioned jealousy again, he'd recognize the symptoms.

He suddenly wanted to kiss her again, feel the pressure of her body against his and her fingers dart across his chest in sexy anticipation. Most of all, he was hungry for her.

Damn amazing.

"Everything okay with those papers?" Marilyn asked as she came into the office.

He looked down at the contract in front of him. "Yes. Why?"

"You usually sign them quickly. But the way you were concentrating, I thought you might have found an error."

Blake picked up his pen and quickly signed the papers, then handed them to his secretary. "Sorry. My mind is somewhere else."

"On Crystal?"

He eyed her narrowly. Marilyn read people—especially him—like a book. "She's something, isn't she?"

"I'd say so. She's as pretty as a picture and twice as nice."

"How do you know?"

Marilyn smiled knowingly. "She brought me a flower this morning. Said I should have one reason to smile this early in the morning."

"Really."

"From what I can see, she took flowers to two or three other store managers too."

"Really," he said again, wondering what she was up to.

"She said it was the least she could do for their help."

What the hell was she up to now? "What kind of help?"

Marilyn shrugged. "Beats me. I didn't have a chance to ask. I've got a tyrant for a boss who says I'm supposed to stay in the office and do my work."

"Unless your work is out of the office."

She ignored his comment. "So I work. Here."

He handed over the signed contracts. "In that case, I suggest you get to work."

Grinning widely, Marilyn shook her head. "Got a doctor's appointment this afternoon, remember? I'm leaving in just a few minutes."

"Who runs this place?" he asked grumpily, still teasing. It wasn't his usual style, but Marilyn was suddenly easier to talk to.

"Mr. Wright, sir," she stated with a chuckle as she left the office. "If you haven't caught on yet, I won't burst your bubble now."

Fifteen minutes later, Blake still had a smile on his face. It was due to relaxing a little with Marilyn, which was due to thoughts of the unconventional Crystal, which was due to her saying yes to a Saturday date with him.

Although he was looking forward to the party with Crystal, he wasn't certain what to expect. But then, nothing had gone wrong between them yet. Probably the worst thing that might happen was that his crowd of social climbers would ignore her. Or that she would ignore them. After all, there weren't any millionaires in that crowd, just a bunch of wanna-bes. So, his guy friends were all safe.

Besides, this wasn't a commitment, it was just a damn date!

CRYSTAL SPENT the rest of the week learning the rudiments of fresh floral arrangements. Designing those were much harder to do than the silk florals.

Silk ones could be rearranged forever or disassembled without any problems. But the fresh ones needed to be handled a little differently, then wrapped in floral wire, taking care not to bend the stems when the flower heads didn't go in the direction she wanted and...the list went on.

"That one will have to be cut to fit there," Linda stated without touching the flower in Crystal's hand.

Crystal picked up another and gave Linda a questioning look.

Linda nodded. "That's a better choice."

"Who knew?" Crystal sighed. "If I had any idea it was this hard to make floral arrangements, I would have tipped like a millionaire when they were delivered."

"If that's the case, the money would have gone to the wrong people. A nice tip is acceptable, but the charged cost covers the designer."

Crystal put the last pink flower in place, then stood back and gave it a critical eye. She wished it looked a little happier than it did. Some of the stems, while not crushed, were decidedly wobbly. "I think I'll stick to silk flowers."

Linda frowned. "I don't understand. You have such a flare for the silk ones. It just doesn't seem to carry over to these."

"I know." Crystal stared at the pink jumble of flowers. "It's just not there."

"It's Helen who can put these together as if they were dropped into the perfect bowl in charming disarray or organized chaos, like an English garden brought into the room. She has the real knack."

"We'd better pray her arm heals in a hurry so she can do them again, or we'll go broke on the ones I create." Crystal looked at her watch. "Oops, I'm having lunch with Dave, the CD store manager. See you after that." She reached for a handful of fresh daisies. "Might as well not let these go to waste. I'll take them as a peace offering."

"I thought you were eating with Darlene?"

"I was, but her love, Danny, is stealing her away for her lunch. And I need a favor from Dave, so I decided not to lose this opportunity."

"Good enough. See you later," Linda said absently as she studied the disheveled arrangement. From Linda's expression, it was clear she wasn't sure what to do with it—hide it or begin again.

Crystal handed a daisy to one of the customers as they entered, then went on her way. She had promised to meet Dave off grounds at a little Mexican restaurant a couple of blocks from the mall. He was a young man who was used to the crazy world of videos, sound bites and instant entertainment. Even when he talked, he tapped a drum beat on the table, the wall or even on his thigh. Nerve-wracking, but she wasn't spending more than an hour with him.

All the way through the mall and out to her car, she realized she was looking for Blake Wright's tall, well-tailored body to walk into sight. She didn't acknowledge that until she had reached the exit and realized that she was disappointed she hadn't seen him. It was a shock for her to admit that she'd actually been looking for him. Conservative, straitlaced, and good-looking Blake had touched her somewhere deep inside. She didn't know why or how, but he had. And now she flirted with his image in her head all day long.

Not good. Not good at all. He was the kind to have his life neatly mapped out. His goals written in stone. His likes and dislikes categorized and filed under the heading of *forever*.

She had her life mapped out, too. Although far more flexible in many areas, she knew what she wanted and he obviously had a clear idea of what he was looking for in a mate. And they didn't fit. Well, they didn't fit as they wanted to. Obviously, something sparked between them powerful enough to make her fantasize about how compatible they might be if they made love—which she wasn't about to do! No sense in complicating the complications.

Besides, she'd made a mistake six years ago, and that was still first and foremost on her mind. She couldn't change it now, but that didn't mean she had to repeat mistakes.

Six years ago, at a young and starry-eyed twenty, she'd been a sophomore in college and thought she'd found her millionaire. His name was Jim and she'd believed that life was perfect. When he'd wined and dined her and taken her to his apartment on the side of the mountain, she'd fallen in love completely. But it had been a disaster. She'd given him her virginity. So much for gifts. After three months he'd dumped her for another woman and the beautiful image of herself as a wealthy society matron was smashed beyond recognition.

It was a good thing she still had her heart.

It took a long time for her to realize that what she thought she'd been in love with was the image of herself as a society matron, not the man who spawned the image. It was then that she knew what she wanted and what she was looking for. She'd be a wonderful, caring wife and mother. She knew how to share and give to people and what made others happy. What she had to remember was that she needed to be happy, too. It was easier said than done.

She could do whatever she wanted and enjoy it, until a man came into the picture. Then she set aside her brains as if she didn't need them anymore. Suddenly she couldn't do enough to make him happy— at any expense. In other words, she put aside her happiness for his.

Wrong move.

She didn't know if this part of her personality was a flaw in general or had come about because she'd always done it with her dad, her hero. And when her parents died, she lost that link with growing up and growing smart. Aunt Helen and Uncle Joe were wonderful, but they weren't her parents. In fact, they'd never been parents before. So, all three stumbled along, trying to do the best they could with the circumstances they had to work with. This part of her life wasn't a topic she discussed nor did Aunt Helen bring it up.

So, for a long time, Crystal stayed away from relationships, hoping she would grow stronger and learn how to please both people in the relationship: the male *and* herself. She was getting there but she wasn't sure enough to trust herself yet.

However, she seemed to feel easy enough and keep her own identity with guys like Blake, who weren't in her life in a personal way. Not personal as long as she didn't let him be. Because she wasn't interested in Blake as a husband, he would be a good subject to practice her new behavior on. That idea provoked lots of good feelings as well as a couple of wonderful images—so wonderful, she felt the bottom fall out of her stomach.

Stepping into her aunt's sedan, she headed across the parking lot in the direction of the restaurant and the young man who was to be her lunch companion.

She could start her practicing on Saturday night. Why not?

Great idea!

"ARE YOU SURE you want to wear this?" Aunt Helen asked. "It's a little colder here than it is in Santa Fe at this time of year."

"I'm sure I want to wear this," Crystal repeated. "And cold is cold once there's snow on the ground. Flagstaff is not too much colder than Albuquerque. Honest." She stepped back into the great room and did a turn around. "Well? What do you think?"

The soft, doeskin moccasin boots she'd worn the first day she met Blake were once more on her feet. But the dress she wore for the indoor picnic was what caught attention. It was an authentic, beaded doeskin Indian dress that came to her calves. Loose-fitting sleeves came to just above the bend of her elbow, and the skirt of the dress was almost an A-line, gently flaring as it passed her hips. The intricate beadwork around the sleeves and neck arrowed down the center bodice.

Crystal's golden hair was straight, hanging down her back in a silken rope.

Crystal watched her aunt's face. "Not your normal apparel for a casual get-together, is it?"

"No," Aunt Helen said slowly. "But outstandingly beautiful on you."

"You don't like it."

"I love it." Aunt Helen looked apologetic. "I'm just not sure how Blake will respond to it."

"Blake will show up in a designer golf shirt, slacks and leather shoes and pretend that it's picnic garb instead of business casual."

"Well," her aunt began, but the doorbell stepped on her word.

"Aunt Helen, you know I'm right," Crystal said as she walked to the door.

Blake looked exactly as she'd said, except for the open suede jacket he wore over it. "Cool," she said, giving him more than a casual look and enjoying his discomforting fidgeting.

"So are you," he said, his eyes resting momentarily on her breasts sculpted by the soft, tan leather. The light in his eyes said she was exactly the opposite. Hot. Very hot.

She smiled, feeling better every minute.

"Blake, is that you?" Helen came to the door, a plum cardigan sweater and slacks set gracing her thin form. A coordinating floral scarf held her casted arm. Her genuinely delighted smile welcomed him. "How have you been? I haven't seen you in a week."

Blake's smile matched Helen's. "I've missed you, too, Helen. Aren't you going to come into the mall and see me? I miss our talks."

Crystal was surprised. Aunt Helen and Blake having talks? About what?

"So do I," Helen stated emphatically. "So why not come by here and let's have lunch? I can open a can of soup or order a pizza."

A pizza? Aunt Helen?

"You're on. How about Tuesday?"

"Wonderful."

Crystal tapped Blake on the shoulder. "Uh, hello? Is it customary for a man to make a date with one woman while picking another up for an evening out?"

Blake looked surprised, but there was a satisfied glint in his indigo-blue eyes. "Jealous? I didn't think that was part of your makeup, Crystal. I'm surprised."

"Well, I'm not," Aunt Helen said, giving her niece a hug. "She's a vibrant and beautiful woman with all the right stuff. And some of that stuff is knowing when an aunt is horning in on her time with a handsome man."

"No, I..." began Crystal. But she couldn't think of anything to say that wouldn't support her aunt's theory. "Darn." She grinned, acquiescing to the assumption they both had made.

Blake said goodbye to her aunt and walked her out the door to his car. "A black Porsche?" she asked, astounded. "What is the world coming to?" She looked from the car to the man, then back again. "The son of a preacher man who can't get away from business clothes and uptight conversations happens to drive a Porsche."

"I like it," he stated, a slightly defensive tone to his voice. Apparently she wasn't the only one who thought it didn't fit with his personality. He slipped into the driver's seat and started the powerful engine.

"That's even more mystifying," Crystal stated.

He placed the car in gear. "I like you, too, but you don't question that."

She felt the warmth of his words race through her blood. "*That* is understandable. After all, I'm different than you are."

"You're supposed to say that you like me, too."

There it was, that staid and mathematical logic of his: one answer equals another. "Of course I like you, too," she said patiently. "I wouldn't be going out with you if I didn't."

"That's nice to hear." He shifted gears. "I feel the same way."

"I'm not in your schedule," she reminded him.

"No."

"I'm not your type."

"Not exactly."

"And you're still here."

"And I'm not rich enough for you."

"No."

"And you're not like the woman I was looking for, either. The rich, preacher's-wife kind."

She looked at him in shock. "You're looking for a wealthy woman?"

Blake hesitated only a minute. "Yes. And you're not it."

She wasn't willing to admit how much that hurt. She wasn't admitting why it hurt, either, especially when she'd just about said the same thing to him. "Then this is the sexual pull I originally thought it was."

"One *big* sexual pull," he stated grimly. "But you already knew that."

"So," she said, sitting back as he rounded a curve. His strong hands handled the wheel as if he were caressing a lover. "What do we do now?"

"I suggest we just relax and let's see where it leads," he said. "Of course it's just a suggestion."

She swallowed hard. "Right. Don't push it." She remembered his hands on her back, his mouth covering hers. The dizziness. The growing ache in the pit of her abdomen.

Her mouth went dry.

Somehow, she wanted more than anything in the

world to be in his arms and to be forgetting how much they *didn't* suit each other. Thank goodness logic prevailed, she told herself. All she had to do was remember six years ago as well as the fact that she was on a different quest. Blake wasn't it. It sounded like a futile call to the Alamo, but it helped.

5

When Blake drove up to the house, the party was in full progress. Music, light and laughter filtered through the front doors.

As they walked through the door, the noise became just a little louder. Not seeing his buddies, Blake possessively slipped Crystal's hand in his and led her through the living area and into the kitchen. He liked the feeling of protecting her this way, although he knew she probably didn't see it the same way he did. The soft warmth of her palm touching his was sensuous, the rubbing of their skin erotic. He clamped down on that thought. The son of a preacher knew how to do that without question.

When they reached the kitchen, he stood for a moment before speaking. Sure enough, several guys were gathered around the stove-top island, beers in hand. Crystal slowly pulled her hand away and he missed it. As he casually placed his left arm around Crystal's shoulders, he surveyed the room. She leaned into him, her blond hair just below his chin, and he felt secure once more.

"What a slow-starting bunch," he commented just loud enough to grab their attention. "Must be numbed brainpower."

"Hey, Blake! Glad to see you!"

"Hey, Blake. I wondered when you'd get here."

"It's about time!"

"Where've you been?"

"Good going, Blake. Late for the second time in a year!"

Blake greeted them all with a handshake and an occasional hug before introducing Crystal. "This is Crystal Tynan. She's visiting here from Santa Fe. And she's with me. Please remember that, and treat her with respect," he stated in a no-nonsense tone.

A dark, good-looking guy walked up, admiring Crystal with his eyes while he spoke to Blake. "Had to go to another state to get a date, Blake? Somewhere they don't know you?"

Blake suddenly wished he had Crystal to himself rather than sharing her with a room full of single sharks. What had he been thinking of to bring her here on a second date? "Don't get carried away Sam," he warned.

His friend still ignored him, feasting on Crystal instead. "How could I? Just because she's beautiful and charming—and with you—doesn't mean I'm in love. Yet."

Crystal gave a delightful laugh and held out her hand. "Hi. I gather your name is Sam and you're friends with Blake."

His eyes rounded. "How did you know?"

"Because he's bigger than you are, and you wouldn't talk that way to him without being close."

"Beautiful *and* smart. A lethal combination."

"Hi, Crystal Tynan." A man with merry black eyes and a gentle way reached out to shake hands. "My name is Cruise, and welcome to the party. Patty, my wife, is playing hostess in the other room, or I'd introduce you to her, too." He motioned over his shoulder to the man who had looked at her so boldly. "Pay no attention to Sam. He's a ladies' man, flitting from one beautiful lady to another."

"Oh, no!" she teased. "My heart is broken by a fickle man again! What are the chances of that happening twice?"

Blake frowned. Who was the first man she thought was fickle?

"Looking as beautiful as you are, the chances are slim to none," Sam stated. "I'm ready to walk a million miles...."

"Enough, all of you animals! Keep this up and I'll leave with Crystal. That will teach you to kid around without a license," Blake growled. But a couple of the men knew he wasn't kidding. That brought another thought. Was he as serious and lacking in fun as Crystal thought he was? Was he really a stick-in-the-mud? Odd, he'd consider that now. He'd never thought of himself as anything but conservative, which, until Crystal brought it up, seemed to be a good thing to be.

Someone slapped a bottle of beer in his hand and handed Crystal a glass of wine.

Crystal was laughing at something Cruise had said. Cruise was beaming as if he'd just discovered the art of scintillating conversation. Blake looked around. Come to think of it, all the guys were attracted to Crystal. Two were eyeing her doeskin-covered breasts. They looked so...tempting.

If he said anything, the guys would think he was a jerk, which he'd be. If he pretended he didn't notice, then he'd be sick with worry in case she was interested in one of them more than in him.

He never should have brought her here. This was like bringing a prize painting to an auction and everyone looking at the piece of work as if they were speculating what it would be like to be the owner.

Suddenly she leaned sideways, and looped her arm through his. "Well, Mr. Wright. Are you going to show me around or do I have to fend for myself?"

Blake smiled. Everything felt all right again. He was back on firm ground and Crystal was with him once more. He felt as if it was him and her against the crowd. Us. A strange wonderful feeling of belonging slipped over him.

He was getting in trouble and he knew it. He just didn't give a damn. Tomorrow he'd worry about his reactions. Not tonight.

With every bit of gallantry showcased, Blake offered her his arm and then escorted her out of the all-male kitchen area into the dining and living area. Several men were standing with their wives in conversations with others.

Blake noticed for the first time that his usual group, the friends he ran around with, were all in the kitchen, isolated from the women. The married guys seemed to enjoy the company of the women far more. Although he knew it wound up that way, he'd never really noticed that before.

"Fear," Crystal murmured.

"What?"

"Fear," she repeated quietly. "Most of the guys in the kitchen are still a little fearful of women. A lot like teenage boys. They don't have one or they've never been in an in-depth relationship, so they hang out together for security."

It was unnerving. How the hell had she guessed what he had just discovered? "Those fearful guys are my friends."

"I know." She gave a little shrug of her shoulders. "But that doesn't change the facts. If anyone should know, you should. My guess is that, except for the host and maybe one or two others, none of them have had or are in a relationship of any depth or length."

"Don't be so judgmental," he stated with far more authority than he felt. "You don't know them."

Her hand tightened on his arm. "No, but I struck a nerve somewhere."

"Not mine," he said just seconds before introducing her to Cruise's wife, Patty.

Half an hour later, with Patty and Crystal deep in conversation with several other guests, Blake went to get both of them another drink from the kitchen. He was in awe of Crystal's instant popularity and more than a little confused. Everyone who met Crystal liked her. No holds barred. She was dressed differently than any other person in there, she men-

tioned to one person that she loved their aura and
told another that he reminded her of the soul of an
Indian spirit god. He'd never heard of such nonsense
before, and thought anything remotely like it was
bunk from some con artist's bag of tricks. But his
friends were lapping it up. Patty had even made tea
so Crystal could read tea leaves like she said her
great-grandmother had taught her.

That thought was a little scary. He'd seen kooks
with those thoughts before, and there wasn't a thing
he liked about them. To his mind they were on the
outer fringes. It was just another piece of ammuni-
tion to remind himself to maintain space between
himself and the woman he brought as a date.

It wasn't easy. Suddenly, he was a hero to his
friends because he brought the genuine hit of the
party. Crystal was so far from the kind of woman he
usually included in these things that most of his
friends were looking at him a little differently, as if
he had a dimension to him that they hadn't seen before now. He hated to admit it, but it felt pretty good.

"Hey, Blake, that's some lady you brought,"
Cruise said as he walked back into the kitchen behind him. "She's not your usual type. Where did you
find her?"

Blake twisted off the cap on a beer, hiding his irritation at his friend's words with the action of stran-
gling a brew. "What do you mean she's not my usual
type?"

"Come on, man. You know what I mean. She's

funny and direct and a little off-the-wall. Not your usual straight-as-a-ruler kind of woman."

"And that's what I usually date?"

Cruise laughed. "Not just yes, but hell, yes."

"Well, you're wrong."

Cruise took a swallow. "No, I'm not, but if you want to think so, who am I to stop you?"

Blake started again. "We're just friends."

"Then stop looking at her as if you want to eat her alive. Then maybe she'll stop looking at you as if she wants you, too."

"She looks at me like that?" Damn, he wished he'd kept his mouth closed. On the other hand, who else would tell him the truth?

"Man, she likes whatever you've got. And so do you. It's written all over you two." Cruise took another gulp of his beer. "Reminds me of Patty and me when we first met. Both of us wanted to do something about it, but we weren't sure what. Neither wanted to make a commitment, but we didn't know what else to do."

They were looking at each other as if it would lead to *marriage?* Blake didn't think so—not for a moment. "She's looking for a millionaire."

"And with the way she sparkles, she'll find one eventually. But she doesn't look the type to be happy with the obligations of that life-style for long," his friend pronounced with authority. "Too much of a free spirit."

"And how did you get so knowledgeable?" Blake asked.

"Easy. Patty was going to marry a millionaire, too." Cruise grinned and held out his hands as if embracing the room. "And here I am."

"Excuse me," Blake stated sarcastically. "But I missed the point."

"She decided to settle for the potential in me, instead."

"You? Potential?"

"You bet. With Patty's brains and my ability to earn money, we're going to make it to a million by the time we retire."

Now Cruise had his attention. Blake was conservative enough to have stowed much of his own earnings away. But he wasn't quite sure how Patty and Cruise were doing it. Blake swung a kitchen chair around and straddled it. "Tell me more," he said, nodding toward the other chair.

Cruise sat down across from him. "Well, first I had to decide what area I wanted to invest in...." he began.

Half an hour later, loud laughter came from the den, breaking up the conversation between the two friends.

Blake looked at his watch and realized he'd left Crystal to her own devices while he and Cruise talked investments. He felt guilty and hoped she wasn't angry with him.

"Didn't mean to keep you so long," Blake stated, pushing the chair back under the kitchen table. "But my respect for Patty has grown twofold. And Crystal reminds me of her. You've got a sharp lady as well as a pretty one."

Cruise laughed. "You're telling me. You know that old expression, 'Behind every successful man there's a pushy lady.' Well, that's my Patty. And I thank God every night."

"You're lucky." Blake meant it.

"Yes. But during the time when she's pushing, I curse a lot," his friend said easily, slapping Blake on the shoulder as they walked out of the kitchen and toward the spot where the group was circling around something—or someone.

Blake's stomach clenched. If his instincts were right... They were. Sam sat backward on a dining room chair just the way Blake had been sitting earlier. His head rested on his crossed arms over the back of the chair as he moaned and groaned with delicious reaction to being touched. The group was clustered around him—and his masseuse. Crystal.

He should have known.

She maneuvered his shoulder blades with a gentle but firm touch, then moved up his shoulder to his neck and webbed her fingers into his hair, gently rubbing the pads of her fingers against the side of his head above the ears.

"Now, if you do this every night for twenty minutes or so, I guarantee a proposal at the end of a month," she promised. Laughter followed.

Sam gave another groan of pleasure. "I promise I'll do it sooner if you don't stop now."

A fist clenched in Blake's chest. Crystal had her

hands on Sam's body and Sam seemed to love it. Sam was enjoying this way too much and Crystal was enjoying it, too. He could tell by the expression on her face. She was a born leader and a truly gifted teacher if her audience was any indication. She had charisma.

Just at that moment, she looked up and saw him. Without stopping, she gave him a wink and went back to her demonstration on how to get a man to propose after seducing him without cooking.

And here was his date, but touching another man. Sam was a ladies' man who counted notches on an imaginary bedpost. Blake ought to know, he'd heard enough of the stories in the kitchen with the other guys...the same guys Crystal said didn't know women very well.

But she knew Sam well enough to touch.

Patty came to his side and stood watching. "You can bring her over any time, Blake. Party or no party."

"So she can keep the men happy?" he said quietly. He'd meant to be teasing, but it sounded just like what it was: sour grapes.

"So she can sparkle the way she's supposed to. She's a wonderful mixer. That's a gift."

"Everybody has some kind of talent, Patty."

"That's for sure, but hers is visible. She makes a party, bringing everyone together instead of allowing you guys to separate." She looked up. "See?"

Kitchen guys. So even Patty had known. It wasn't

that Crystal was the first to notice, she was just the first one to comment to him about it.

Blake was learning.

But the jealousy that grew like a giant ball of grease in the pit of his stomach wasn't going away.

"Now this is a technique that feels good to both parties," Crystal said, placing the heel of her palms against Sam's temples, then gently increased the pressure.

Sam groaned again.

"If I do this too hard, I'll scramble his brains, so I can only do this to a point." She grinned. "Darn it."

More laughter.

Blake walked away. The conversation continued to buzz around the room but he needed to get away before he said something really stupid. He walked out the kitchen door to the backyard, reveling in the chill of the day. He needed the chance to cool off and figure out what his problem was.

Within seconds, he knew the answer. It didn't take brain surgery to figure it out. It was Crystal. He wanted her in his arms and in his bed. He wanted sex with her. Good. Fun. Romping. Satisfying sex that made him sigh loudly with contentment afterward. That was it.

No, he wasn't thinking marriage, like she was talking about during Sam's massage. They were too opposite. Besides, he needed to be with a woman who was more like him—neat, subdued, far-thinking. Someone who didn't make friends with everyone who came her way. Someone who didn't incite riots by being so damn sexy. Someone who would never drive him into doing things out of jealousy or temporary insanity.

On the other hand, he was too attracted to Crystal to leave it at that. He wanted her to the point that it was interfering with his sleep. Just the thought of his kissing her after lunch the other day was enough to make him more than ready to make love to her.

He was as randy as a goat.

The chill finally penetrated his shirt and pants, and he decided to donate his presence to the party. The food was about to be served.

Meanwhile, he'd developed a train of thought to follow. It was a simple plan, really. He'd let Crystal know that he didn't appreciate her touching other men while she was his date. Then he'd forgive her for not knowing it wasn't polite and then...then he'd take her home and drop her off. Next week, he'd ask her out again. Maybe to dinner. Then, he'd slowly ease his way into making love to her.

But he wouldn't get any more emotionally involved than he had to. After all, this wasn't a permanent relationship. She wanted a millionaire in her life, as if that would heal all ills. And Blake wanted someone a little more...conventional. Someone who thought he was the greatest thing since man was made.

For the first time, he realized he wanted someone who loved him beyond belief. He wondered what it would feel like to have a woman treasure him.

CRYSTAL LEANED BACK in the seat and gave a contented sigh. "I enjoyed your friends, Blake. They were all very nice. Especially Patty. She and I had more in common than I dreamed. Why, we were almost soul sisters." She looked at him. "Have you known them long?"

"I knew Carl from a Cleveland mall. When I moved here I looked him up. He introduced me to Cruise and the rest, and we've all been friends ever since."

"Really?"

"Honest." He cleared his throat. "Where did you learn all that hocus-pocus?"

"What?"

"You heard me. All that aura, spiritual crap that goes along with reading tea leaves."

"If I thought you were going to insult me, I would have stayed home." Her voice was quiet, reminding him to curb his frustration.

"I'm sorry. I didn't mean to hurt your feelings. It's just that I don't believe in it."

"But your friends aren't quite as closed as you are." It was a friendly reminder.

Damn. "That's true. But I want to ask you a favor. Please don't do any of that hocus-pocus stuff around me anymore."

"I'm sorry," she said, her tone full of regret but steady just the same. "I can't do that."

"What?"

"I can't stop being who I am. So if you want me to be someone else, then I suggest we don't see each other any more," she sighed. "I'm sorry about that, because I think we both have enjoyed this... this...whatever it is."

He wasn't quite sure what he'd heard. "You won't refrain from that stuff when we're together?"

"No."

He couldn't believe she'd said no. She'd refused his request. Just like that. "No? Just like that? No?"

"No. Because I'm sure you see that it's a part of me. And you wouldn't want me to really deny a part of myself. It would be like asking me never to be a masseuse. And I know you wouldn't do that, either. And I also know that you wouldn't want me to not be true to me. Well, my spiritual beliefs are a part of me." She smiled. "I know you understand what I'm trying to say so ineptly."

"Well..." he said dryly. "I think you've found a way to get it all out."

They drove in silence for several blocks, then reached the main cross street. Crystal gave a sideways glance and smiled. "This is interesting."

"What's that in your voice?" His own tone held a hint of irritation.

Apparently she'd struck a nerve, Crystal thought. So he was far more touchy than she'd assumed although she wasn't sure why. His friends were honest, down-to-earth and interesting. He was a part of that group. So, aside from being terribly sexy, he also had to have attributes like his friends. The fact was, he was no follower. He was a leader and that kept him just slightly apart from the rest. She answered decisively. "A little disbelief that you have friends who are so open to new ideas. And maybe just a little anticipation at seeing you loosen up a little...with me."

Blake pulled the car against the curb and stepped on the brakes. A streetlight was directly over them, shining on the front hood of the sleek auto. "What?"

She leaned toward him, narrowing the space between them and laughed softly. "You heard me. I want to see more of you, but we both have to be willing to accommodate each other more. Get along better."

"Like how?" he asked suspiciously. Just the words *see more of you* conjured images that teased him more than a blatant proposition stated aloud could.

Crystal tilted her head as if thinking. "Well, we both know that we are attracted to each other," she began reasonably. But just the thought of those words made her heart beat faster. "We both know that we're not really what the other wants, but we're attracted anyway. And whatever this chemistry is, it's still there after almost two weeks."

"True." He leaned back, but his narrowed eyes never left hers. Light poured through the windows, shadowing her high cheekbones and beautiful eyes. "What do you suggest?"

"I suggest we get to know each other better."

He had a few thoughts in that direction himself. "Why don't we start now?"

She looked as startled as he perpetually felt when he was with her. "Now?"

He smiled. "Why don't we start by having coffee together. Just the two of us. Then we can discuss this further and see where we go from here."

He was scrambling her brain. It wasn't responding. "Coffee?"

It didn't matter that she was a kook. At least he knew what kind of kook she was. It was manageable...for the moment, he decided quickly. Blake leaned over and placed a chaste kiss on her parted mouth. He touched her hair, feeling the silkiness of it against his palm. A man's hands and mouth could get lost in that feeling. *This* man's hands. "Coffee. Maybe with a little brandy."

"Where?"

"My place."

Her eyes widened as she studied his face

He prayed his lustful fantasies weren't *too* evident to Crystal. He was only a man, and his daddy had told him that men thought of sex every ten seconds. But for the sake of their souls, men didn't act on it. Blake was also in charge of his body at all times. Well, most of the time, he amended. He didn't seem to have quite as much control around Crystal.

Her long lashes dipped to brush her cheeks, then rose again and allowed her to look into his soul. A small smile formed on her mouth. "We aren't compatible, you know."

"I know, I know," he said, his voice more rough than he meant it to be.

"We really are opposite."

"We really are," he agreed, still rough-voiced.

She looked sad. "This attraction won't last."

"I hope not." And he meant it.

"But you want to explore it for the moment anyway."

"Yes." There was no hesitation.

Even though it was past midnight, her smile lit the car with the golden glow of sunshine. "I'd love coffee."

Purposely restraining himself, he leaned forward and gave her one more chaste kiss. He had great intentions. But, her palm stroked the side of his face and he lingered a moment longer, then one moment more. His body immediately responded to her touch.

Crystal's hand dropped and he stiffened. With more restraint than he believed he'd ever shown, Blake pulled back and stared down at her.

Her eyes held a deep, dreamy quality he could fall into. Her hair cascaded around her shoulders like a halo. "I never knew coffee could be so addictive."

"Neither did I. But I'm willing to explore that taste further if you are."

"I am."

Placing the car back in gear, he eased back to the street and began the trek home. Suddenly he wished he'd chosen an apartment much closer to his friend's house.

A glance to his side underlined that wish. Crystal sat next to him, her hand on his thigh as she stared straight ahead. There was a small smile that played around her sweet-tasting mouth, but her thoughts were someplace else, too.

His heart was thumping so hard it reminded him of when he was a kid and climbed a tree. He'd been elated when he got to the top limb until he'd looked down. Then, his heart had jumped into his throat and with each thump it had closed off his breath. He had been barely able to move, unable to see anything except the thin carpet of leaves on the ground below. Adrenaline had flowed through him like tiny, combustible rockets. It had taken him an hour to get down, but he'd been thrilled for weeks afterward—just like he'd known he would be as he'd stared out at the countryside.

Only right now, he was on one big rocket heading into the night sky.

They pulled into the parking lot of his apartment complex and drove to his own garage. The outside parking lot was almost empty. The younger crowd was still out and partying. Midnight was still considered early to them.

Carefully parking, he got out and went around the passenger side to help Crystal out. But she'd already opened the door and was stepping onto the concrete floor.

He smiled. "You were supposed to wait."

"I don't know why. I don't wear hoops, I haven't got on high heels, I'm not wearing a corset that would impair my breathing."

He took her hand and helped her out. "It's customary to allow the man to help."

"Silly custom."

His arm circled her waist, and he realized again just how fine-boned she was. She had very feminine curves in all the right places, but she wasn't plump. "Independent."

"Chauvinist."

They walked to his apartment and he opened the door.

As far as apartments went, it was nice. His furnishings, although masculine, were in excellent taste. Tan leather couches with a matching chair and ottoman took up most of the living area. A round glass table with matching tan leather chairs were in the adjoining dining room. Paintings were hung in groupings on the walls and there were some interesting sculptures on the glass tables. She didn't have time to stop and look, he was right behind her nudging her along.

But she stopped after passing through the hallway into the living room. Everything was formal, but it was a cozy formal. "I love it. It's warm and homey." She gave a quick smile. "And not a business suit in sight."

He smiled back, recognizing her teasing and not jumping to the bait. "Thanks."

Crystal dragged her hand from the leather of one chair to one of the bronze sculptures. "Intriguing texture combinations."

"Thanks again." Blake turned to get a bottle of wine from the rack behind him.

"Blake?" Her voice sounded light, hesitant.

He stopped and turned. "Yes?"

She stood quietly in the center of his living room, looking both proud and vulnerable. Her wide brown eyes watched him. Her Indian costume blended with the color scheme as well as she did. Her hair, slightly mussed from his hand and the brisk wind, was like a halo around her piquant face. The ache that had begun earlier in the pit of his stomach grew with want. She looked so womanly, yet so very vulnerable. A single wrong word from him could crush her spirit. Funny, he'd seen her so many times, but this was the first time he realized that. He felt instantly manly and protective.

She tried to smile, but it disappeared quickly. "No coffee."

"Wine?"

She shook her head, her eyes never leaving his face. "Make love to me?"

It took a moment for his heart begin its heavy thud again. He straightened up and slowly walked toward her until he was directly in front of her.

Her small face looked up at him as if there was nothing else in the universe worth looking at.

"Are you sure?"

"I'm sure."

"No regrets later?"

"Only that we didn't meet sooner."

He shook his head as if to brush her humor away. He was doing everything but laugh. "I want you, Crystal. I won't lie. But I'm not promising anything."

"Neither am I, Blake. I just want you to make love

to me." She was honest and sincere. He saw it in her eyes. In her stance.

His hand shook as he touched her hair. "With pleasure."

Her sigh echoed in the room. Her warm breath touched everything, including his heart....

6

BLAKE WRAPPED his arms around her waist and pulled her easily but inexorably toward him. With studied slowness he brought their bodies together and held her against him.

Bending his head, he brushed his mouth against her temple, then grazed down the side of her cheek. With hands that shook, he cupped her face in his large palms and finally placed his lips against hers. The tense waiting was over—or would be soon enough. Every muscle in Crystal's body eased with the thought. At that moment, she'd never wanted anything as much as she wanted Blake.

From the moment they'd met, she'd been drawn to him. In the course of the past week, it hadn't changed one iota. It had just gotten worse—much worse. That ache in the pit of her stomach had grown enough to consume her every thought and want and need, jumbling all together until she didn't know her own mind anymore. Even tonight at the party, she'd looked for him whenever he'd disappeared. She'd waited for his return, only feeling like smiling when he was around. Everything else she said and did was just going through the paces.

It was the *man* she craved, not the act.

Crystal reached up to stroke his jaw, then allowed her hand full rein as it drifted down the column of his throat to the broad, strong chest beneath her hand. His heartbeat thudded beneath her palm, telling her he felt the same things she was experiencing. He wanted her, too. Thank God.

With breath that could barely grab air, she kissed him back. She didn't want to hold her feelings in any more. She wanted to experience everything with this man. Everything that brought them closer together for this moment in time.

Suddenly she wasn't close enough to him. She wanted to feel his flesh rubbing against hers, his hands touching her skin, the weight of his body on her, meeting, stroking and filling her with his very essence.

Instead, just when she needed him the most, Blake backed away. He dropped his hand to clasp hers. "Come," he said, his voice sounding like coarse sandpaper.

With a solid step, he led her into the unlit bedroom. Blake stood her next to the bed, which was masculinely covered in a gray-tan-and-black spread. His blue eyes stared down at her as if he couldn't get enough of seeing her standing by his bed.

With shaky hands she reached up to the back of her doeskin dress.

"No," he said, his hands tightening on hers. "Let me. I want to undress you."

It was a good thing she didn't speak, because she couldn't think of one thing to say. His slow smile lit up her heart. She had wanted to make love to Blake since the moment she saw him standing in the doorway of her aunt's shop. It had nothing to do with love, she told herself. Nothing at all. Besides, love at first sight was only a writer's dream, not reality. She and Blake were the poster people for opposites attracting, and that didn't lead to any more than a fling. This feeling was nothing more than chemistry—very strong chemistry—and she was smart enough to know the difference.

But it didn't detract from reveling in his touch. Blake turned her around and slowly began unbuttoning the back of the dress. The silence in the room was so deafening she could hear her own breathing. She also heard Blake's and was so glad he sounded as starved for air as she was. One by one he unbuttoned her doeskin buttons until she felt the cool night air tickle against the small of her back.

He stroked her bare shoulders, feeling the frailness beneath his hand. "Turn around," he said hoarsely.

She did as he asked, staring up into his face. Warmth flooded her limbs, making her feel wanted and needed and so very feminine. His gaze was as heated as fire, sensitizing her for his touch.

Blake reached up to her shoulders and brought the neckline to her shoulders, then edged the dress off. It fell quickly, slipping off her arms to puddle on the floor. She stood in her black lace bra and panties, holding her breath and waiting for him to say something. She was more full-figured than the thin beauties she imagined Blake was used to. He probably thought of her as fat in this day and age. Maybe he wanted someone who was as thin as the anorexic models in magazines. Maybe he saw her appendix scar and was turned off by it....

"Say something, Blake. Anything," she begged, her voice low. "I need to hear your voice."

He smiled slowly. "You're so very beautiful, Crystal." His finger touched and trailed across the top of her bra from one breast to the other. "Your skin is so soft."

Suddenly, everything was all right again. "I'm glad you think so." She reached up for the buttons at the throat of his knit shirt. "My turn," she said as she slipped the hem out of his waistband and ran fingers underneath his shirt to slip it off.

But Blake was far more impatient than she was. He needed no more encouragement. Instead, he took the hem of his shirt and pulled it over his head, dropping it to the floor next to her dress. Then, with a clasp that was both gentle and firm, he pulled her against the wall of his chest and buried his face in her hair.

"Dear gentle heaven, you smell as sweet as clover and taste as good as angel food cake."

She gave a low laugh. "You sweet-talking devil." Reaching between them, she managed to unbuckle his belt and unsnap his slacks. Crystal laughed again, this time in triumph. "Victory is mine." She sounded breathless.

"And mine." He slipped off the slacks, then

reached behind her to unclasp her bra. Then, with a blend of awe and wonder, he cupped her heavy breasts tenderly in the large palms of his hands. "So beautiful."

He bent his dark head to taste the lusciousness of them, one at a time. Savoring, tasting, stroking. Crystal cradled his head and watched him, studied his sculpted mouth, feeling such intense pleasure and immense power, all mixed together.

His mouth drifted from one breast to the other, then came up to claim her mouth once more.

Slowly, they drifted onto the feather-filled spread. Lying side by side, they touched and sipped and loved one another. Tears formed in Crystal's eyes with the beauty of his lovemaking. He was strong, but so very gentle. Hard and firm, sweet and giving. His words were sweet to her ears, telling her how very wonderful she was. She felt precious and treasured and all the things she knew love was meant to feel. And she loved Blake all the more for his knowing the words her soul needed to feel nourished and expansive.

And when he entered her, Crystal was mindless with need. *Blake. Blake.* She hadn't realized she'd said it aloud until his mouth covered hers and swallowed the words whole.

His hands melted into her hair, weaving his fingers through the soft ropes. Holding her, tugging her, needing her. When he pulled his head away, it was reluctantly. "Now, Crystal," he rasped. "Now, darling. Give it up. Come on..."

And she did.

So did he. She felt herself spilling over the edge of the rainbow and plunging into sweet, blessed nothingness. Floating in his arms.

When she returned to the softness of his bed, she opened her eyes and stared up at the ceiling. Blake's head lay next to hers, his lips softly breathing kisses on her cheek and ear. "Mmm, so sweet. So very sweet."

Happiness flooded her being, just as the tension and release had done a moment before. She grinned, then the grin turned to laughter, spilling into the silent apartment like sweet rain after a drought.

Blake looked at her with a bewildered frown. "What's the matter?" he asked warily.

"Absolutely nothing!" she proclaimed, tightening her arms around his back and feeling his muscles. "You're wonderful and I'm wonderful and we're wonderful."

His brows rose and the tension around his mouth eased. "That's it?"

Still laughing, Crystal placed a light kiss on his chin. "That's it."

"You're sure? Nothing is wrong?"

"I enjoyed us. You," she said softly, "are wonderful." Her gaze took in the indecision in his eyes. He was worried about his performance. It was so like him. Big, bold bluster on the outside and such a sweet, vulnerable teddy bear inside. "You're the one who made things right."

Obviously relieved, he smiled, finally getting

caught up in her happiness. Giving a soft laugh, he rolled over and curled next to her, his hand wrapping around her waist to pull her close to him. "You think so?"

"Of course. I'd never say anything I didn't mean."

Blake pushed a loose strand of hair away from her face. "I'm glad to hear that."

She closed her eyes and enjoyed his touch. The feel of his hand draped across her waist, his leg covering hers. His mouth, close enough to reach up and touch, was temptation indeed. In fact, everything about this moment was perfect. She wished she could stay this way for a long time.

That thought startled her. This wasn't the man to have those thoughts about!

And he wasn't looking for someone like her, either. She was too open, too volatile, too easygoing and spiritual in a way he didn't understand. And mostly, too uninhibited with people—namely his friends. Her life-style was far less structured than his. He was so methodical, so precise and conservative. So...darn good-looking.

That was it. This attraction to Blake was just a passing fancy.

Her smile disappeared. She was as reluctant to let go of this moment as she was afraid of becoming attached to the man.

Blake's mouth brushed her cheek, her eyes and then brushed her parted lips. "What's going on, Crystal? What are you thinking?"

Her voice quavered. "This is just for now, right?"

He missed a beat, then picked up with the light brushing movement again. "Right."

"It's for fun and because we're so attracted to each other."

"Right."

"And it isn't forever."

"No, it's not forever, Crystal."

"Just until I leave to go home."

"Just until then."

One tiny tear escaped the corner of her eye and he caught it on the tip of his finger. Her breath caught in her throat and she fought to keep her emotions at bay. This wasn't the time for tears and she didn't even understand why she was crying. "It wasn't a tear."

He smiled. "No. Of course not."

"I don't cry."

"No, I wouldn't imagine a woman like you would ever be that vulnerable."

"I'm not vulnerable. I'm happy."

"Would you make me happy?" he asked in a whisper that was as naked as their bodies. "Again?"

He had done what she couldn't do; distracted her enough to stop the rest of the tears. She smiled and touched his full mouth with her finger, outlining it before placing a kiss there. "I'd be happy to," she said softly.

SITTING IN CHURCH next to Aunt Helen Sunday morning was a lesson—but Crystal wasn't sure which lesson it was. It could have been any one of so many....

Blake hadn't driven her home until a little after three in the morning. She'd been very quiet tiptoeing through the house until she reached her room. Then she'd plopped into bed and slept soundly for five hours until Aunt Helen woke her to attend church. Crystal could have turned her down, but knew it was probably where she needed to be. Besides, since her Aunt couldn't drive with her broken arm, she had no way to get there without Crystal.

When they returned home, she'd sleep like a cat on the windowsill. Until then, she was scared to close her eyes for even a moment for fear of falling asleep and embarrassing herself and her aunt. Instead, she focused on the young minister and tried to make sense out of his words. Her aunt gave her an occasional quizzical look and she would look alert for all of a moment, before going back into her semi-awareness.

As for an explanation, she certainly couldn't tell her aunt what she'd been doing all night that had made her too sleepy for church! Besides, she had a little praying to do.

CRYSTAL AWOKE from her afternoon nap and stared up at the ceiling. She had dreamed of making love to Blake. His body, so beautiful and well structured, was a memory that would remain an active image in her mind even after she was on the rocking chair on the porch of her Southern mansion. Even in her old age, she'd remember the way the dim light played off Blake's magnificent body.

She should have known he'd be as particular about his muscles as he was about his clothing.

And his face, so intense and yet gentle...

The sound of his laughter interrupted her reverie. Her own smile returned. Then she frowned.

Blake? Laughter? Was she hallucinating?

Crystal jumped up and opened her bedroom door a crack. She peeped straight down the hallway to the living room, but couldn't see a thing. But she could hear her aunt's voice and Blake's.

He was here. Here!

Her heart beat quicker. She closed the door, then raced to the Hollywood bath and ran a brush through her hair. She added a touch of lip gloss and mascara, then tried to compose herself before leaving the room. She was cool and calm and collected and ready for anything life threw her way. She was Woman....

She heard Blake's deep laughter again just as she reached the end of the hall. He was sitting at the bar, a tall glass of iced tea in his hand as Helen filled the miniature theater-popcorn popper to make a new batch.

With a smile still framing his face, he turned to see Crystal standing in the doorway.

Her eyes ate up the sight of him. Knowing what was beneath his clothing, her gaze wandered over him. He was still dressed in business casual. It was probably the most informal he ever dressed. A pale-blue knit shirt and darker blue slacks fit snugly over the trim, athletic body she'd dreamed about earlier.

But his eyes were what drew her attention. Although his laughter still tilted his mouth, his eyes spoke of the same hunger she'd just felt awaken inside her.

She wanted to be enfolded in his arms, to feel the security of his hard body as she rested her head against his chest. She needed to have her arms around his neck, to touch his cheek, feel his heartbeat against her breasts.

Instead, she said the only word she could think of. "Hi."

"Hello."

"Hey, honey, look who's here," the older woman said to her niece. "I had to go to church and pray before Blake would bother to come visit."

"Now, Helen, you know that's not true."

"Maybe not, but I'll get some mileage out of that before I give it up," she teased.

Crystal walked into the room and stood at the bar beside Blake. She felt all fingers and thumbs. She was out of breath yet couldn't walk a straight line across the living room.

Blake's hands were splayed over the counter and she stared at them. They were the same hands that had touched her so knowingly and intimately last night. The same hands that had...

"Crystal?" Her aunt's voice intruded.

She blinked. "Yes?"

"Are you all right?"

Crystal laughed, pushing her long hair behind her shoulders. "I couldn't be better. Why?"

"I was talking to you and you kept staring at the counter."

"Oh, I'm sorry!" Crystal thought fast, hoping the blush she felt on her cheeks wasn't as noticeable to others. "I was daydreaming about an arrangement I'd like to try."

"Linda told me you were very talented in the silk arranging," Helen said. "Do you really like it as much as she thinks you do?"

"I love it." That was the truth. She did. It brought out her creative side and gave her great satisfaction when an arrangement was sold. "It's a new creative outlet for me and one I wouldn't have expected."

"Really?" Blake said, stepping into the conversation. His voice rumbled, causing every nerve in her body to vibrate in response to that sound. "I would have assumed you'd be good at it right away. You have such an, uh, unusual creative knack."

She couldn't keep the blush from heating her face. It felt as if she'd lit a blaze.

Blake smiled.

Helen looked closely. "Are you sure you're all right?"

"Just a little flushed from my sleep, Aunt Helen. Honest." She looked over the counter. "Popcorn. I love it."

"Good. It's one of the few things I can make with one hand," Helen said. "Not quite an elegant appetizer, but, an attempt at civility."

Laughter eased the tension in the air, and Crystal relaxed. This was Blake, the man she'd thought enough of to make love to. And that was far more rare than even he knew.

And it was her aunt, who was almost as close as her own mother had been. In fact, she'd practically taken over the job when her mother died. Both had lost best friends then, and both had become more close than usual for aunt and niece.

Most people rightly took Crystal for a free spirit. It was more than her openness proclaiming her unusual ideas. It was because of her straightforward conversations, odd dress and the way she looked people in the eye and demanded respect. Most especially, men weren't used to that. She wasn't much of a flirt, but she was always stunned when men reacted to her by making advances. Many had tried. Few—less than few—had succeeded. Until Blake.

Amazing. And Blake didn't have a clue that she wasn't sure what she was doing last night. He probably thought she knew everything there was to know about sex and love and tingling bodies.

Whatever he thought, Crystal didn't want Aunt Helen to know about their making love.

"I'll get some salt," Helen said, coming around the bar area and heading for the kitchen. "The butter is already melted in the container."

The moment she left the room, Crystal turned to Blake. "Don't say anything about last night!" she whispered.

"What would I say, Crystal?" He grinned. "'Geez,

Helen, your niece is great in bed!' Or 'I can't wait for tonight when Crystal comes to my place for a sleep-over. By the way, you don't mind if she spends the night again, do you?'"

"Here we go!" Helen said carrying a large bowl with a salt shaker in it. "Almost ready for a treat."

"By the way, Helen, did Crystal tell you about her new project?" Blake let the last word hang in the air for a moment before continuing, and Crystal stiffened, ready to stop whatever he was about to say as soon as he said it. "She's taking on the task of decorating your windows."

Helen filled the bowl with popcorn, then put it in front of them and sprinkled salt on the popcorn. "She's told me about a few of her plans and I told her about mall regulations."

"Maybe I'd better go over them with her." He grinned. "I have a copy of the lease at home."

"Oh?" Crystal asked. "Do you have a bottle of wine to go with it, Mr. Boss Man?"

"Certainly you don't need a whole bottle, do you?" Helen's voice held a ring of mock shock.

"A glass or two would be nice."

"I can do that."

"This is a work night, Blake. I need my beauty sleep," Crystal warned.

"You're beautiful whether you sleep or not." His voice was low, as he forgot for a moment that Helen was in the room. "And I promise I'll get you back in plenty of time for your second nap."

Crystal's heartbeat accelerated. She could spend

the afternoon and evening with Blake. The thought was captivating. Wonderful. Wicked.

"Why don't you bring your suit and we can swim?" Blake suggested. "We can show you what New Mexico is missing."

"It's missing your April heat," Crystal commented dryly, but she wanted to say yes with all her heart.

"I think it's a wonderful idea," Aunt Helen said. "Just be home at a reasonable hour so you can get enough sleep to open my store on time."

"Will do," Crystal replied, excitement coursing through her veins. She stood and aimed for the bedroom. "I'll just get my suit."

"I've got a couple of thick, fluffy towels you can use," Blake stated as she left the room.

But she already knew that....

7

IN THE COOLNESS of Blake's apartment Crystal suddenly felt awkward and uncomfortable. Was he expecting...? Should she...?

"Let me get that glass of wine," he said, stepping into the kitchen.

Music flowed out of several speakers from the corners of the room. Classical. She should have known. "Do you always play your stereo when you're gone?"

"Always." His voice was muffled. "I like coming home and hearing it. Makes me feel welcome."

"Classical."

"I can change it to rock or jazz." He came around the kitchen entrance and raised a brow in question. His hands held two crystal glasses of golden-colored wine.

Unwilling to look into his dark-blue eyes, Crystal accepted one and turned toward the patio doors. Although it was January and the temperature was chilly, sun poured through the vertical blinds warming the apartment. The trees outside the fenced patio were bare, waiting for spring to clothe them. Beyond them was the apartment pool. But her mind was focused on the man standing near her. She was aware of his presence with every fiber of her being.

"Crystal, what's on your mind?"

She took a sip of wine. It was a delaying tactic. "Nothing, why?" She looked up at him and knew she was lost.

The intensity of his gaze ate her up at the same time it filled her with heat. "You haven't lied to me before. Why start now?"

Her breath came out in a soft whoosh. "You're right," she finally admitted. She was torn between being afraid he'd march her to the door, or worse yet, that he'd laugh at her. But she had to take a stand. "I guess I'm just scared. I want to make sure that we understand each other. I mean..."

"No ties?"

That sounded so...unconnected and made what she had experienced last night sound trashy. It wasn't—not by a long shot. But she wasn't sure what to call what she wanted from Blake. All she knew was that she'd never been so scared. "Well, not any more than a dating couple would have."

He stared at her a moment.

"No permanent ties?"

"Right," she said, relaxing.

He tilted his head, those piercing eyes boring into her as if they were drills. "Afraid of commitment?"

She looked him straight in the eye. "Only with someone who's not right for me."

His gaze narrowed. "Are you telling me I'm good enough to screw but not good enough to marry?"

His voice was low, growling at her. The sound of his voice was enough to scare little children from the door. And the chill in his eyes was as deadly as an avalanche.

Tension filled every nerve in her body. Marriage? Where was he coming from? "Are you asking for marriage?"

"No."

She relaxed. Even though she knew it sounded wrong, she had to stand up for what was best for her. No one else would. She took a sip of her wine, wishing she had the nerve to gulp it down. "I'm telling you that we're not meant for marriage. You and I both know that. But there's this chemistry thing...."

He looked puzzled as he studied the problem. "Let me get this straight. After last night, you're telling me you'd like me for a stud but not for the long-term."

"It's a coarse way to put it, but—" she tilted her chin up as if she were tilting windmills "—yes."

Every man's dream. His slow grin was as wolfish as it was sexy. "Well, then," he said, taking her glass away from her and setting it down on the table along with his. "You can't complain, then, if I take my job seriously." He put his arms around her waist and tugged her closer to him. "After all, we've only got five more weeks before you go back to Santa Fe."

Thank goodness, he understood how incompatible they were. She felt the relief of her words being voiced aloud and agreed with. But, somewhere deep down, she felt the implied rejection of not being good enough to marry. To be Mrs. Blake Wright. She tried to ignore it. Whatever that feeling was, it didn't need to be analyzed. She'd said what she needed to, and was still where she wanted to be: in Blake's arms.

She placed her hands around his neck and pulled his mouth toward hers. "Then you'd better be good, Blake. We've only got five more weeks to make this relationship perfect enough to commit to memory."

His laugh was rough and low. "Something to remember for old age?"

He was closer to the fact than he realized. She kissed the tip of his chin, then planted kisses all over his throat and neck. "When I'm old and gray and sitting in my rocker on the porch of the nursing home, I want your image to pop into my mind and bring a smile to my lips."

"Instead of your husband's?"

"Instead of my childhood."

And she kissed him as if there was nothing else on her mind but the two of them making love. It was the truth.

But somewhere, in the back of her mind, a part of her was laughing at her naiveté.

BLAKE HELD CRYSTAL by his side as she lay with her eyes closed, her breathing slow and easy. Finally. For the past hour she'd teased and tempted him. He would have bet that she'd felt their coming together as deeply and profoundly—almost as much as he did.

Crystal moved and his arms automatically tightened. She was asleep and he didn't want to have her out of his arms. Not yet. Time enough. Time enough...

He pushed away thoughts that didn't please him. He was a man, and men were accused of not paying attention to the details of emotions often enough. He was just following the pattern, he told himself.

Years ago, right out of high school, he'd been married. It had been to a girl he'd known the last two years of school and he had felt he was ready for marriage. He'd wanted to be with someone. All his life he'd wanted someone to think he was special. His parents had tried, but they had been so busy saving souls, sometimes they had forgotten their son's needs.

So he'd married. For the first several months they'd played at house as if they had nothing else to do. It had been a wonderful time. He'd never felt lonely and she'd been a playmate in every sense of the word. They'd played at dinner, they'd played with their friends and debated politics and other issues they'd had no knowledge of. They'd started college and had played at that, too. Most of all, they'd played at sex.

By the time a year had passed, they'd realized that playing wasn't getting either of them anywhere, and, with the help of their parents, they'd settled into getting a college degree. It hadn't taken long for both of them to realize that, besides a bunch of old high school friends and memories, they didn't have much else in common. Within two years it had been all over but the shouting. She'd gone on to become someone else's Mrs., and Blake had completed college and gone into the corporate world. No hard feelings between them.

But he'd never forgotten those first few months when they'd shared a total and honest connection that took away the feeling of loneliness.

But he didn't trust it, either. Knowing that they'd had it and still hadn't been right together, he'd become even more withdrawn and solitary, relying on no one but himself. It was easier that way.

Real estate was like a game to him. It was challenging, as was this management team put together by a New York corporation that owned twenty-two malls across the country. A few more years and he would be with the big boys in corporate headquarters. He couldn't wait. It was the challenge he was looking for, tasting it on the tip of his tongue. Success. Just a few years away.

But in the back of his mind, he was loath to admit, he wanted to share this traveling up the spiral staircase to corporate America's door with a companion. A spouse.

He realized Crystal was not that spouse. Neither of them had any illusions concerning that issue. They were as different as ditch water and the ocean. But that didn't keep the attraction from forming. She was right. They weren't meant for each other for the long haul. He knew it. He agreed with it. He just wished she wasn't so damned adamant about it.

She could *pretend* to be reluctant to end their affair. But pretending to be something she wasn't was as foreign to her as designer labels.

Thinking of pretending brought another thought to mind.

Because of Crystal's openness, Blake had assumed she was far more sexually experienced than she really was. She wasn't. Not at all. What she lacked in knowledge, she made up for in enthusiasm. It wasn't an act, he was sure of that. But every move, every action was a giveaway that making love was new to her.

Last night was an eye-opener. Instead of being delighted, he had to admit—at least to himself—that it made him want to protect her. She was too vulnerable. Too sweet. Too honest. The world could swallow her whole in a heartbeat.

She moaned and Blake looked down. Her eyes were still closed, but her tongue came out and sipped at his pebble-hard nipple. His body responded instantly, becoming rock hard and ready for this woman in his arms.

Her hand trailed down his chest, arrowing toward the part of his body responding most to her touch.

"Mmm. Are you awake?" she murmured.

"I am now," he growled.

"Good." Her voice was edged with satisfaction. "I'd hate to take advantage of you when you don't know it."

Blake chuckled. He loved her sense of playfulness. He loved her honest reactions.

He rolled over and captured her body beneath his. "A physical impossibility."

"Really?"

"Yes, and I'll show you why," he whispered, making love to her one more time.

WHEN BLAKE opened his eyes, he found Crystal, head propped on one arm, watching him with her incredible doe eyes. A smile formed as he blinked.

"Hi." Her voice was soft and warm.

"Hi, yourself." He didn't move in case she did. And he didn't want her moving an inch.

Her smiled widened. "I need you to get up and take me away from all this."

"To where?"

"Sedona."

"Now?" Was she crazy? By the time they got there, the sun would be setting. He'd rather stay right here with her in his arms.

"I want to see the sunset."

That explained it. "Couldn't you see it from here?"

"No." She gave a playful slap to his stomach and stood. He was thankful for all those months of weight lifting. If it impressed Crystal one little bit, it was worth every minute of working out. "Come on, big boy. Stun me with the beauty of it."

"I thought I had," he groused, finally seeing no way to back out of her crazy plan.

Crystal was dressed in less than a minute. Blake couldn't believe she just threw on her clothing and was ready to go. It took Blake a little longer to do the same thing.

She watched him as if he were under a microscope, her gaze wide in awe.

Giving a sigh, Blake turned and faced her, hands on his hips. "Spit it out, Crystal, before you choke on it." His voice was patient.

"Wow, I'm just amazed. I didn't know a man could be that particular about how a knit shirt is captured inside the waistband of his pants."

Blake narrowed his eyes. When he gave his intimidating Clint Eastwood stare to most people, they closed up.

Crystal began giggling. With that spontaneous, infectious laugh of hers, she wrapped her arms around his waist and gave him a hug. Just a hug. But it felt as if she'd given him the gift of a slice of heaven.

Blake enclosed her in his arms and rested his cheek against the top of her blond head. There was no urgency or surge for sex. This was a communion of souls that felt as cleansing as if spring water were washing over him and soothing the blistering heat of the sun on his emotions.

After reveling in his touch, Crystal moved her head to look up at him, her face still wreathed in a smile. She kissed the tip of his chin. "You're adorable and I think you're wonderful just the way you are."

He couldn't believe she was so quick to make him feel terrific. The woman had power!

"Thank you." He still held her in his arms. "Let's go."

"Okay." Her arms rested on his chest.

"Now or we'll miss the sunset."

"Let go." Her tone was sexy-soft and sweet, and reminding him they couldn't go anywhere like this.

He did it reluctantly and took her hand, leading her out of the apartment and into the car.

It was too late to take the scenic drive through Oak Creek Canyon to the dramatic red soil and rocks of Sedona. Instead, Blake took the freeway, pushing the speed limit but not driving one mile over it.

Crystal brushed her hair quickly, with long sure strokes. "Do you always do things by the book?"

"Explain," he said, watching the car behind them in the rearview mirror as it pulled off the side of the road.

"I mean, are you always this cautious?"

He looked over at her and was immediately occupied with wondering what it was like to brush a beautiful mane like hers. He also knew exactly what she was talking about. "Yes. There's nothing so important to get a ticket over. A ticket costs a hundred dollars for maybe getting there five minutes ahead of time. When I make a hundred dollars an hour seven days a week, I'll think about breaking the speed limit." Damn! He sounded so stuffy!

She hesitated a moment, thinking it over. "That makes sense. Especially if you're already investing in some kind of stock pool."

"Thanks," he stated dryly, but he felt good about his opinion anyway. But just to show her he wasn't quite as stuffy as he sounded, he shoved the speed-ometer up two miles past the limit.

She made no comment but Blake knew she'd noticed.

"Have you ever been here before?" she asked.

"When I first moved to Flagstaff, I came with a group of friends. Have you?" he asked.

"Yes, the first time was with Aunt Helen, who knows her way around here as if she built it. And I love it."

Helen? She didn't seem to be the type. And Blake knew her husband had been rather straitlaced, too. It just didn't fit....

Within a few minutes he pulled off the highway toward Phoenix and aimed for Sedona. It wasn't long before they saw large monoliths of brilliant-red rock that looked as if they had grown toward the sky to greet whatever gods the Indians had worshipped. Long shadows etched dark flames on the ground as the sun began its nightly ritual.

"Turn left," she said, her eyes darting everywhere as she sought out something.

"Where are we going?"

"To a vortex."

"Vortex?" It sounded vaguely familiar, but he wasn't sure what it meant here.

"The Indians believed this ground was sacred. There are supposed to be several places where the magnetic pull is stronger than at any other place in North America. It's a place to gain energy and release from chronic pain."

"Do you believe that?" he asked, taking the next turn she indicated.

"Does it matter? I'm just telling you what is said. It's up to each individual to believe."

"That's hedging your bet," he stated.

"Pull over here," she said, smiling at his discomfort but unwilling to snap at his bait. "And let's walk for a few minutes."

He looked at her as if she were crazy. It was about fifty degrees out there and they hadn't brought coats. It was also getting dark and she was talking mumbo jumbo. "This doesn't sound like a good idea," he began.

"You came this far, Blake Wright. Traveling two miles over the speed limit, I might add. Why not go the rest of the way on this adventure?" She glanced out the window. "The sun will set in another ten or fifteen minutes. What is so important that you'd sit in the car to hold on to?"

Damn she was good. She almost made sense. That irritated him more than going over the speed limit had. He refused to say the word that was on the tip of his tongue: *you.* But Crystal wasn't his to lose. This was just one of those interludes or encounters in life that will change with time. The time being Valentine's Day...

"Let's go."

Fifteen minutes later, they reached the first mesa by a path that led to the top. Crystal took his hand and led him to the edge. "Look," she said, smiling as if she'd given him a gift.

She had—a gift he would long remember.

Beyond the tree that had shaded them when they first reached the plateau was the most spectacular sunset Blake had ever seen. Oranges, brilliant and soft, yellows, cobalt-blues turning to washed out sky-blue, pinks that rivaled the blooms of a hundred roses; they all streaked across the sky to swirl into the most beautiful palette ever created.

"Damn," Blake said under his breath.

Crystal gave a low chuckle, stepped in front of him and placed his arms around her waist. She leaned against him, the top of her head barely touching his chin. "I've only seen it one other time, but it's stuck with me for the past ten years. Isn't it the most beautiful thing in the world?"

Feeling the smallness of her waist, the warm clasp of her hand over his, and the natural perfume of her body mixed with the scents of their lovemaking and the desert view, he knew he could name a few other beautiful things. "Yes."

They stood enfolded in each other's arms for twenty minutes or more while God changed the palette of colors, shifting and turning them into a moving rainbow until the light was almost gone and the sky turned a vivid gray.

Then, without words or hurry, Blake turned her in his arms and kissed her.

It started out as a thank-you-for-the-sunset kind of thing, but, instantly, it went much deeper than that. Mouth gently parted mouth, then arms entwined through the others as Blake pulled her into the hard planes of his body. His hands had a will of their own, tracing her spine and hips and feeling the wonder of their softness and resilience. A sheet of lightning laced the sky, and then came the loud boom of rolling thunder. Reluctantly, Blake pulled away.

Crystal's eyes were open but dreamy. *He* had put that dreamy quality there. Blake Wright. All by himself. And that fact made him as proud as he'd ever felt.

"I don't know which is better, you or the sunset," she murmured, all of her brown-eyed attention on him.

"If you don't know," he teased, "then I didn't do it right."

Her eyes widened at that, but she never said a word. Instead, Crystal gave him a smile and took his hand in hers again. They climbed back down the rocky path to the side of the road where they had parked the car.

But once inside, Blake kissed her again.

"Now do you know?"

"Yes, but I'm not talking," she said in a low voice.

"Why not?"

"Because you might stop attempting to convince me how terrific you are," she admitted honestly.

His laughter filled the car. The feeling of warmth stayed with him all the way home.

An hour later, they were back at his apartment. Blake ordered pizza to be delivered. When it arrived, Crystal organized the plates and napkins.

But after serving the pie slices, she sat on the floor

in the living area and looked out the window at the dark. Her gaze was locked on the trees outside, a dreamy look on her face. She had a beautiful profile, but he wished she were looking at him the same way she was looking at the trees. He was pretty sure he wasn't included in her thoughts.

"What are you thinking?" he finally asked.

She turned around and looked at him in surprise. "Why?"

"Because you're so quiet and you're usually so vocal."

Grinning, Crystal held up her plate. "I'm eating."

Although she smiled, Blake still felt left out. He was reminded of that feeling of communion he'd had earlier—the same one that had reminded him of his first marriage. He must be sick if he thought communion came from sex. Wasn't he old enough to know it took time and effort and love to make that electrical connection? Or was he too damn old to know that on more than a surface level?

"I'm getting old," he muttered, disgusted with himself for even entertaining the thought of having that feeling with Crystal. Not just because of who Crystal was, but because of who he was, too. Where was his judgment?

"You are not." As if she knew what he was thinking about, she answered, "You're becoming wiser. Less judgmental."

"You've been spying on me," he declared.

"Of course." Crystal reached for another piece of pizza, then doctored it with red peppers. She looked so intent upon what she was doing, but he knew better. Her mind, never idle, was going a million miles a minute. Obviously, it wasn't centered on him.

Blake wanted to talk about something that brought her thoughts back to his presence. He couldn't believe it; he was jealous of her thoughts! He wanted all her attention. All the time. A pretty impossible want unless he intended to drain her dry at the same time.

He waited as long as he could before saying something.

"What are you thinking about?" he finally came out and asked. He expected a lot of things, but he hadn't expected her answer.

"The window design I'm going to begin creating tomorrow."

It wasn't the answer he'd expected at all.

Blake had a feeling he was being paid back for all those times he'd taken women to bed and then wanted them to disappear or go home or be quiet. Those times he'd gotten closed into his own world and had thought of all the business things that needed to be done, located, written or handled. He'd basically turned his back on the woman while he did his own thing, patiently—sometimes impatiently—awaiting their leaving.

Crystal was doing the same thing to him. He bet he could disappear for the next hour or so and Crystal would barely notice.

Damn! He hated that.

Paybacks were hell.

THEY STOOD in the middle of the exclusive men's store as Crystal contemplated his clothing: gray suit, white shirt and blue-and-gray tie. "You need more color."

"How much more color?" Blake asked warily.

"Oh," she said airily, "just a little more. Maybe your shirt."

"I like white shirts," he stated, ready to staunchly defend his taste. "They're my favorite."

Her eyes gleamed mischievously. "What about ties?" she asked sweetly. "Do you have any other colors?"

Before he could help himself, Blake looked down guiltily at the tie he was wearing. All his ties looked the same. According to Crystal, they would all be dull. He knew it. Everyone, especially the sales personnel had told him so. But a small part of him had to hold on to those colors. Bright colors might make him look like a fool. "Lots of them."

"What's your brightest color?"

"I don't know." He looked around at the racks and racks of ties. "Bright blue, I guess."

"Are you guessing or is that a fact?"

"Don't second-guess me, Crystal."

"Then be specific."

Damn. It irritated him that she always had to have the last word. "Bright blue." He stated it with certainty. As if it were true. "Besides, I like this."

"No, you don't," Crystal said, flipping his tie. "It's easier for you to wear this than to wonder what colors go with other colors."

"That's not true."

"Yes, it is," she said calmly, reaching for another tie and holding it up to his shirtfront. "This is perfect."

Blake looked down. It was bright yellow with small tan dots that held a smaller dot of blue inside each one. She was right about it being just right and he hated that. But there was no way he could have gone over to a tie rack and picked out the exact right tie. That rankled. "It's loud."

A young woman walked by, but not before she appreciated the colors with her eyes. And her smile. And she was dressed as if money was born to her. Damn.

"One tie. That's it."

"And maybe one shirt," Crystal said, coaxing a smile out of him. The woman was a minx. A fox. A contemporary with opposite tastes. Good tastes.

"Maybe one, but only one," he said.

Crystal smiled. "Just one," she agreed.

He knew he was digging in his heels, but he couldn't help it. He was in charge of his life and his closet and he didn't have to give control over to some woman who believed in tea leaves! "As long as we understand each other."

The expression in her eyes let him know she understood better than he wanted her to....

8

AFTER SUCH a wonderful weekend with Blake, followed by a workday afternoon of shopping, Crystal hadn't gone to sleep last night until several hours after midnight. Instead, she'd curled on her side and thought about the comforting feel of his touch. And then of being able to sit and eat in silence while she worked through a few problems without him demanding constantly to know what was going on inside her head. He didn't need constant attention or baby-sitting like some guys she'd dated. That made her feel even closer to him...and scared.

It was better not to think too much about it, because then she'd become involved with him in more than a time-out-of-time kind of way. And that couldn't be.

Once in her aunt's flower-and-gift shop, all her attention was on her sketches of the front display window. It was a fun challenge to come up with something new and different that would attract the eye and make people smile. She'd played around with several ideas, but finally, with a burst of creativity, she thought she had it. It would be eye-catching and thought-provoking. It was also made for people who had an odd sense of humor.

While Linda watched the store cash register, Crystal gathered the decorations she had begged and bartered from other store managers. Customers came and went, but those who stopped and bought had to be helped first. A usual busy day, it took half the morning to get everything into one location and begin the project itself.

She tore into the old window, stripping down the old decor and setting it into a pile before cleaning the window area itself.

"Sorry, Crystal, but lunch comes first," Darlene said, standing just outside the window area door. "You promised it was your turn to pay again, so I'm not letting you off the hook."

She glanced at her watch, realizing she'd lost track of time. "If you get some takeout and bring it back here, I'll pay for it and we can eat in the window."

"Sounds different," Darlene said with a smile. "Knowing you has certainly been that." She waved. "Be right back."

Twenty minutes later, Crystal and Darlene were eating spicy Thai in plastic containers and drinking tea from large cardboard cups. Framing them from behind was a large blue-and-white vase filled with tall-stemmed yellow and red hollyhocks.

Darlene swallowed her food and pointed to Crystal, who was sitting cross-legged. "You look like a female Buddha," she teased.

"Good." Crystal was delighted. "I like that image. Thank you."

"At times I think you're just as wise."

"I like that, too," Crystal said, smiling at one of the customers who had just stepped out of the shop.

"However, your style is very sparse," Darlene managed to say without a giggle. "There's nothing but us to catch the eye."

"We seem to be doing a good job, anyway, don't you think?" Crystal maneuvered chopsticks as if she'd used them all her life. "More people are paying attention to us sitting here right now than looked at the window all of last week." She waved at a little boy who stared into the window as if it were a small box of delights. His parents stood by him, looking for all the world like the proud parents of a genius. "Maybe we ought to eat in here every day. We'd draw a crowd."

"Sure, but it would take so much work. Before you'd know it we'd be having to coordinate our clothing so we didn't clash," Darlene stated.

"Good point. Strike that idea."

"Can you do mime?"

"No," Crystal said, catching the eye of another couple and waving. "Wish I could." She looked around. "There's barely enough room here for a massage table. But maybe..."

"Don't even think about it," Darlene threatened, knowing her friend was teasing. "The guy walking up to us now would have your tush in a sling if he thought you'd do that."

"Guy?"

"Mr. Blake Wright." Darlene nodded in the direction of Crystal's back. "As we speak."

Crystal looked over her shoulder and saw him coming. Blake was dressed in a dark-blue suit, tan shirt and...was that their brilliant-yellow tie? Yes. Brilliant-yellow. Very unlike himself. It was the one she'd talked him into.

He stopped, his smile quickly changing to a frown. Crystal waved at him. "Hi, there," she mouthed.

"What are you doing?" the words came through the glass dimly, as if underwater.

"We're having lunch. Care to join us?" Crystal asked, holding up her plastic container.

His frown turned deeper. "What is this?"

"Hot and spicy."

He shook his head. "You're not supposed to be eating in the window."

She pretended she didn't hear him. Surely he wasn't going to get all uptight again. "I can't hear you."

Blake motioned that he was going around the doorway and to the window where he could talk to them.

"You know, he's crazy about you."

That her friend would notice it made her happiness level go up even higher. She couldn't keep the grin from her face. "For the moment."

"Moment, moment," Darlene said. "He's crazy about you and I daresay you're crazy about him. Why not get together?"

Just then, Blake stuck his head around the window entrance door. "This isn't right, Crystal. The window is to be used to sell goods for every store. The mall contract states that good taste is to be used."

"And I am using good taste, Blake," she said reasonably. "I'm in slacks and a sweater, and my hot-and-spicy food tastes great, as well."

But he wasn't about to be deterred from his original goal. "You know what I mean," he said. "Step out of there until you're ready to decorate."

"I'm ready to decorate, Blake. Loosen up. This isn't the most shocking thing in the world to happen in a window. Why in Amsterdam..." She hesitated, teasing him into remembering that nothing was shocking, just different.

But he wasn't buying. His one-track mind was still on track. "This isn't Amsterdam."

"You're a stick-in-the-mud, Blake."

"You can call me anything you like as long as you're out of the window," he said, his dark brows forming a thick bridge on his forehead. His mouth was rigid.

Darlene looked tongue-tied.

Crystal stepped in with nonsense. Her hand reached out to smooth the ridge. "Darlene thinks we make a nice-looking couple. So do I, now that you're taking a chance and wearing bright colors."

The tension eased a little...not a lot. "You noticed the bright color."

"Of course, and it looks wonderful on you."

"Colors?" Darlene asked, looking at his clothing as if they were both insane. "Except for that spot of yellow, he's not wearing colors."

Blake was still frowning. He didn't see anything but the contract and wasn't going to let it go unless Crystal moved out. It was apparent he wasn't changing his mind.

"We're talking about the yellow," Crystal said patiently as she gathered some of her meal on the chopsticks and held it out to Blake for a taste. She was so proud of his accomplishment. "Blake's not usually so wild as to add a splash of brightness to his conservative wardrobe."

Blake was not to be dissuaded. He stepped back and held open the side door. "Out." It wasn't a request. It was a demand.

Nothing like ice water to douse any daydreams of eternal bliss. She ought to be thanking him for this. Instead, she was too irritated. Crystal gave a heavy sigh and slipped the chopsticks back into the container. She gave Darlene a look that said it was time to end the window picnic.

But the young woman was still amazed at the color her friend thought was brilliant. "*That* spot of yellow is a bright color?" Darlene asked incredulously as she unfolded her legs and stepped from the window. She was obviously not believing they were talking about the same thing.

"Well, yes," Crystal defended as she stepped from the window. No matter how hardheaded Blake was, she had to be fair when it came to his first attempt at color. "It's a start." She looked at Blake, thinking yet again that his stubborn adherence to rules without question was one of the biggest differences between them. "Are you happy now?" she asked him belligerently. "We were having fun and you knew the exact thing to put a damper on it."

"Behave yourself," he stated sternly. "And get the window completed. It's supposed to be empty only one day."

"Then maybe I'd better make the best of it and go borrow some store's naked mannequins to fill the space."

"And maybe I'd close your store down."

"Meanie."

Blake gave her a stern look, then strode out the door.

If she wasn't so angry, she'd be laughing. He looked so out of place when he'd stuck his head in the window. At the same time, he was frustrating. Did he have to be so uptight?

"I hope he dreams of the Thai food he isn't tasting." Crystal smiled sweetly. "And wishes he'd smiled more."

"Mr. Wright likes spicy food?" Darlene asked, more confused than ever. "And not spicy colors?"

"He's changing as we speak, but apparently not quite as fast as I hoped," Crystal stated glumly. "And he's filled with little mysteries. One of them is always contradicting the others."

"I guess," Darlene said slowly, still a little surprised.

"That's what I'm doing, but it's not getting me

anywhere." Crystal knew she was right. She couldn't figure him out yet. Damn the man!

"You two are so perfect for each other, balancing the other out. I mean, he's loosened up so much. Why, he even smiles now, although not this morning. Wow. Ain't love grand?"

That last sentence felt like ice water thrown on her. She had to explain. She had to show that it was not anything at all like the way it looked, despite what Darlene said. "This isn't love."

"Then what is it?" Darlene asked, giving her a look that said she knew what she saw, and it was what she said it was.

"It's..." Crystal paused, looking for a word that would work and coming up empty-handed. She struggled some more. "It's lust."

"No." Darlene looked at her as if she were crazy. "Get out of town!"

"Well, we're good friends, too," Crystal hedged.

"Good friends, my... I don't believe it," Darlene finally said. "I know what I saw, and it's obvious in his eyes and in yours."

"No," Crystal began. But it wasn't as convincing as it had been earlier. Suddenly she wasn't hungry anymore. She'd lost her appetite thinking that she and Blake looked like they were in love. It wasn't in the cards...or in either of their best interests to fall in love with each other. They both needed completely different things from a relationship and had discussed it already. And the past fifteen minutes had proved that. If eating in a store window was off-limits, how many other areas she hadn't even explored could possibly be as well?

Lots and lots. No. This relationship couldn't be. A woman has the right to choose her own destiny, and Crystal knew what was best for her.

She would retain her cool and still be friends with Blake, but they would never, ever, get together in a long-term way. Never. She had chosen unwisely to have a grand affair with a man who could never be her partner for life. They'd finish this out somehow—she didn't know how—and then they'd go on their own merry ways. But not together.

Five minutes later, Darlene was gone and Crystal began working on the window display in earnest. She put everything she had into the project, putting all her brainpower into it. She didn't want to think about Darlene's comment or her own mistakes.

Besides, it wasn't true. She wasn't, hadn't and wouldn't fall in love with a man who couldn't be part of her life in a way that she wanted him to be.

Therefore, it wasn't to be. Period. End of story.

TWO DAYS LATER, after much hemming and hawing, Blake and Crystal had reached a temporary truce. Warily, they came together again, but it wasn't the same as it had been before. The camaraderie was gone and he missed it.

Just to show how much he believed in her, Blake had picked up Crystal from work and they'd gone shopping for a new suit—for him. But instead of buying a suit, she'd sweet-talked him into buying slacks and a jacket. The faded maroon jacket was in linen, the pants in a dark tan, and both made by a designer he'd never tried before. It was amazing how changed he felt wearing it. Very jazzed. After alterations, the outfit would be ready in the next couple of days.

He walked into the mall and took the route that allowed him to pass Helen's store. What he saw made him stop in his tracks—the senior citizen Mall Walker Club was already in the mall in force—and it looked as if most of the seniors were standing around the store window. Even this early in the morning, apparently it had turned into a social stop, for many were talking to others about the weather or dates or exercise. Intuitively he knew there was something outrageous in that window.

But what had originally stopped them from their rounds was the window. Blake stepped up behind them and peered between heads and shoulders to see what had caught their eyes.

Thousands of roses, carnations and mums sat in crystal bowls as if they were the most beautiful of arrangements. More were tied into lavish bouquets, wrapped in various colored papers, attached to the papered wall behind and hung from the ceiling with whimsical, brilliantly colored ribbons and bows. Although perfectly decorated and lavishly presented, all the flowers were dead or dying.

Crystal slipped inside the window to add another ribboned strand of flowers, and his eyes popped. She was wearing a fitted white T-shirt and a black, bodysuit that hugged every curve and hollow of her lush body. Her long blond hair was pulled back from her face and worked into a massive braid that hung down her back like a rope as thick as a man's wrist. Stray tendrils delicately curled around her hairline at forehead and temples.

She placed three professionally painted signs at the base of the arrangements. One said, Don't You Wish You'd Enjoyed Their Brilliant Blooming? Another said, The Gentle Laughter Of Flowers Makes Joy. And yet another said Time Is Short. Bring Beauty Into Your Life Now.

Very unconventional and nothing he would have approved of, had he been asked. But since when would Crystal ask him for an opinion? No matter what he said, his advice seemed to be the worst thing she could hear. He would have advised her against this window dressing. It was too much of a downer.

All last night while they were shopping she had been planning this window and had refused to let him know what she was up to. She knew he wouldn't approve.

And he didn't. It was bordering on bad taste—though no doubt Crystal thought otherwise.

But he couldn't deny the effect it was having on the crowd. From the conversations he was overhearing it seemed to be reminding people that they had unfinished business in all areas of their lives. As for being an attention-getting, thought-provoking window, that it most definitely was.

Crystal turned around and smiled at the crowd,

but her eyes never met his until she was about to leave the window. When she finally spotted him, she gave a delighted bold and brash smile that lit up the entire window. It touched him somewhere deep inside. To top it off, she winked. Right in front of everybody.

Blake wanted to curse under his breath. As much as he tried to act as if it happened all the time, an embarrassed flush tinged his tan. The crowd turned to look at him and smiled. He smiled in return, even though it probably looked like he was eating persimmons. At the same time, he couldn't understand how he could feel such pride at being singled out in public by a forward young woman who looked as if she were doing nothing more than flirting.

He hated to admit it, but he wanted more. More of what, he wasn't sure.

As he returned to his office minutes later, he still felt the one emotion that claimed him overall: he felt pride. The woman in the window had seen him, chosen him and he felt like a winner.

Embarrassment be damned.

THE SHOP was crowded with customers all day. Helen dropped by and got stuck behind the cash register, but she didn't seem to mind at all. Around eleven o'clock, Crystal dialed Blake's office.

"Did you bring jogging clothes with you?" she asked when he answered the phone.

"I've got some workout clothes in my trunk. Why?"

She grinned as if seeing him. He was so eager—and so wary. "Thought you might like to go to a smaller mall and do some walking."

"What time?"

"Forty-five minutes."

"I'll pick you up," he stated. "Be on time."

"Promise," she answered before hanging up. Meeting Blake was just for the exercise and conversation and someone to keep her company, she told herself. But secretly, her heart sang with joy anyway.

In fact, during the next couple of weeks, her heart sang a lot. Helen came into the shop at least once a day, staying for a couple of hours at a time. She usually timed her "helping visits" during the lunch hour to overlap with the employees coming and going. It freed up both Linda and Crystal, taking off some of the pressure and time constraints. It also helped keep Crystal up-to-date with the bookkeeping.

And in between working and insuring her aunt was fed and happy, she saw Blake. As much as possible.

But there was a bittersweetness to their love affair. They both knew it had no future beyond Valentines's Day, when she returned to her own world and he remained in his. It *would* end.

All her life, Crystal knew she had to marry a millionaire to live the rest of her life the way she wanted. Life was a compromise, and she was willing to compromise in order to have the mate of her choice.

She'd once read a university study that had researched happiness. It had come up with the top ten things that had to do with attaining that elusive state, which seemed to be the one thing people most sought in life next to food and shelter. According to the study, the number one requirement for the attainment of success and happiness was to pick the right mate.

Crystal believed that with all her heart and soul. Her parents had been two of the most wonderful people she'd ever known. Still. And she'd idolized them both. But their arguments had been legendary, their tempers flaring and ebbing like the tides. And usually, the one argument that had rung out over and over had been the one that solidified Crystal's belief in her own theory. They'd argued about money. How to spend it, how to make it, who spent more, why one spent more, how to spend less, how not to spend at all.

The fights had been endless, going on for days, then retreating while occasional bouts of loving had taken their place. But in no time the fights had revived. Anything could set them off, from grocery buying to a new bedspread or a pair of shoes. Her parents' constant fighting had bled into every aspect of their family life. She had been almost thirteen when the fighting had been tragically ended. Her parents were killed in a car crash. A passerby had told the police that when he'd passed them just moments earlier, they had been arguing loudly, with hands flying in the air and words heard over the sound of traffic.

Crystal was sure the topic had been money, just as it had been ever since she could remember.

Dear sweet Aunt Helen and her husband, Joe, had stepped in. Even though Helen was her mom's twin sister, she was so very different. She was calm, quirky, dependable and had a wicked sense of humor. She had shown Crystal how to save and what to spend. She had presented the other side of the money argument, stating that as long as one was frugal in the right areas and learned how to make it grow, one would always have money. And no, little Crystal, it didn't hurt to marry it.

Her uncle Sam had backed Helen in whatever the lesson given. Quietly, he'd backed everything Helen did, including loving her and making her laugh.

When Crystal had been seventeen, Aunt Helen and Uncle Joe had moved permanently to their favorite place, Flagstaff, Arizona. They'd visited the city every year ever since Crystal could remember. It was only right that Uncle Sam retire where he wanted to, where he'd built his dream house. But Crystal had been old enough to stay in Albuquerque, New Mexico, where she had lived her whole life with her parents and aunt and uncle. After attending college for a year, she'd become interested in massage therapy, and decided to give it a try. It had turned out to be something she enjoyed and had brought in money for college. However, she'd never returned to college.

Instead, she'd devised a plan to ensure security. She needed to marry a man who loved her, wanted children and who had the ability to ensure her children's inheritance and well-being.

Although she cared greatly for him, Blake could not ensure enough money to give her that lifetime of security she needed.

"Damn." Her voice was soft, but the sentiment was right on target. She didn't want to admit just how badly that thought hurt her heart. She wasn't willing to think of the future without Blake, either. Nor did she want to believe she was in love with him.

One glance at the calendar on the wall told her it would be only two weeks before she headed back to Santa Fe and her jobs; one as a masseuse and one as the searcher of the perfect man for her.

Blake stuck his head in the door of the store later that afternoon. "How about jogging in the park with me this evening?"

She grinned, refusing to allow all those feelings of woulda, shoulda, coulda interfere with the next two weeks with Blake. "I've got other plans, Mr. Wright. Pick me up at Aunt Helen's around six this evening, if you don't mind."

Blake's eyes lit up. "If you insist. What are we doing?"

"You'll find out when you get there. Meanwhile, wear that jogging suit."

"See you then," he said before walking out of the store and heading toward the back part of the mall. He had an appointment with some major store representatives and would be gone all afternoon.

"Boy, he's got it bad," Linda stated with satisfaction. "And so have you."

"Nope," Crystal said quietly, not wanting her Aunt Helen in the back room to overhear her in case she had the same thought. No sense building up false hopes. "We're just good friends who like to fly kites together."

Linda looked stricken. "Kites?"

Crystal nodded. "Kites. Of course, he doesn't know it yet, but I'm sure he'll enjoy it."

Linda's eyes got even wider. "This is the same man who has run this shopping mall with an iron fist and a smile as tight as—" she hesitated "—as tight as can be?"

Laughter spilled from Crystal. She was having as much fun introducing Blake to the wonders of cheap fun as he was learning to do things most kids knew about by the time they were ten years old. "That's the same man. He's not as tight as he used to be."

Helen came around the corner and caught the last of the conversation between her niece and employee. "You two are good for each other."

"It's temporary," Crystal said, reminded of the window dressing incident. It would happen again, she was sure. She grinned. "I certainly believe that when I'm gone, he'll remember me."

"Long after you're gone, honey," Helen said. "Maybe you ought to stay so you can *really* teach him a lesson."

Crystal dusted off one of the display tables, then sprayed the glass with cleaner. Her heart beat quickly at the notion of staying, but she also knew where her happiness lay. "Sorry, Aunt, but my heart lies in New Mexico."

Her aunt's gaze was penetrating, but Crystal ignored it by continuing to clean.

"What does New Mexico have that Flagstaff doesn't have?" Linda asked curiously.

"Work in less than two weeks." Crystal wasn't willing to admit that it was more than that. New Mexico was the only home she knew. "My furniture. My clothes. My job. My opportunity."

"You can have your furniture, your clothes, your job and your opportunity right here, Crystal Tynan." Helen looked her straight in the eye.

Crystal sighed. Lately this had been the pattern of conversation. Her aunt was relentless. "I like it where I am, Aunt Helen. You know that."

"You like the type of clientele," she corrected softly. "I thought I taught you that security was inside us all. Not in someone else's bank account."

Crystal reached for her purse under the counter. Grabbing it, she swished her long hair over her shoulder and stood straight. "I'm taking a break. I'll be back in fifteen minutes. Does anyone need anything?" Her smile was bright but a fire lit her brown eyes.

Aunt Helen came from behind the counter and reached around her niece with one arm, giving her a light hug that dissipated some of the tension in the air. "I'm heading for home," Aunt Helen said softly. "But I think we need to have a talk."

"Oh, we will, Aunt Helen. Just not now," Her voice was as firm as her aunt's but her face still showed frustration and anger. She knew she had to cool off somewhere first. The sad thing was, she couldn't understand her own up-and-down emotions herself, let alone discuss them. It seemed that lately she was in a state of flux. Happy to sad in a roller-coaster minute could have been her motto. The closer it got to the time to leave, the worse the highs and lows were becoming.

Within minutes she was out of the store and walking with purpose down the mall, circling around the window shoppers and children, her German sandals making a soft, slap-slap sound on the marble flooring.

But the thought that ran through her mind, blocking out the anger and frustration took every bit of her concentration.

By Valentine's Day, she'd be in her own apartment in New Mexico. It was important to remember that. This time in Flagstaff was only an interlude. Her apartment and job were awaiting her there. She had to get tough so that, when the time came, it wouldn't hurt her beyond belief.

After all, Blake wasn't in love with her, either, or he would have changed more, loosened up more, been more responsive to their differences and celebrated them....

It wasn't love, it was lust, and it was never highlighted more than now.

9

SPREAD OUT ON Patty's kitchen table was the financial section of the newspaper with the latest Dow Jones and Nasdaq listings. Crystal pointed out several rising stocks to Patty who was looking over her shoulder. The foursome, Patty and her husband Cruise, and Blake and herself, were all going to dinner together. Little had she known when she met her that there was so much she and Patty had in common. An interest in stocks for one. Patty and Crystal were in the kitchen discussing investments while Blake and Cruise were in the living room watching a soccer game on cable TV as they all waited for the baby-sitter to arrive.

Patty studied the listings in front of her. Crystal had checked off several stocks. "This is so cool," she said. "I've invested in mutual funds until now, and I've done pretty well. But this is the other kind of investing I was searching for."

"I know what you mean. Everything counts when you're trying to make money. My problem is that I don't make enough to invest as much as I'd like."

"What about investment clubs? Do you belong to one?" Patty asked.

"Not yet." Crystal grinned. "But give me time and

I will. I've taken several extra courses at the college on finances and such, though," Crystal admitted.

"So have I." Patty laughed. "Cruise gets concerned when he sees me sitting at the kitchen table working our investments at night instead of watching TV. He thinks I need time to relax, not realizing that having enough money to pay bills ten years from now and to afford a college education for the kids is what helps me relax."

Crystal had never run into another woman who felt quite the same way she did about security. That wasn't the only way they were similar. In fact, meeting Patty had been like finding a soul sister. "Believe me, I understand," she said.

Crystal and Patty bent over the listings once more, comparing stocks. Crystal only dimly heard her name called as she hunted for a couple of her stocks.

"Crystal!"

Blake's voice finally reached her. She looked up to see Blake with Patty's husband standing in the doorway, coats in hand. "Yes?"

"It's time to go." His voice was a little softer.

Cruise stood at the kitchen entrance with a grin on his face and his wife's coat held out for her to slip her arms into. "Come on, babe. I'm taking you away from all this for the night. You can work on it later, after we make love and I pretend I'm asleep so you can get out of bed and do more studying."

Patty giggled as she gave him an elbow in the rib. "Shame on you, discussing our sex life in front of others. Besides, you don't pretend. You are dead to the world."

"See what a gem she is?" Cruise asked the ceiling. "She's so honest she can't even go along with a joke."

"We've been married ten years, Cruise. Your snoring is no longer a joking matter."

Crystal folded the newspaper, her attention caught in the conversation—finally. "Ten years? That's a long time."

Cruise laughed. "Not when you're aiming for sixty-five or seventy anniversaries together." He wrapped his arms around Patty and planted a kiss on the top of her head.

"We're just babes in the wood," Patty confirmed. "But we're working at keeping it an enchanted forest."

Crystal watched the two of them, envious of the obvious love between them, even after all this time. She craved to be loved like that, to feel so secure in the love she'd helped create. She glanced over at Blake.

His indigo-blue-eyed gaze locked with hers. His were fired with blatant frustration and anger. Why? She'd given him everything she was capable of giving. More than she had wanted to and that she would give again to someone she didn't intend to marry. Ever.

They'd been together five weeks. One more week to go. She'd never given so much nor received such rewards for giving. Blake was one uptight bundle of wonderful surprises. The best surprise was his ability to catch on quickly and loosen his own grip on staid behavior. He was loosening up more each day.

Was her effort enough? Was it too much? Or was something else about her making him unhappy? Was he embarrassed that she was only a masseuse while he was climbing the ladder to corporate success?

What had she been thinking! Her gaze darted around the room as if searching for an escape. Blake wasn't the man for her! They had already decided that they were nothing more than a diversion for each other—an important interlude, but an interlude nonetheless. He was to practice upon, not devote herself to. He wasn't anywhere *near* being the New Mexico millionaire she'd been seeking! He wasn't even willing to allow her to be her uninhibited and unusual self, while *he* thought being dressed in suits with a dollop of yellow in a tie was outrageous!

She and Blake were so different, that after the first blush of newness wore off, they would fight over everything. Constantly. And that was no way to bring up children. Ever.

Little ones needed love and attention and esteem and fun times and attention and lots of sisters and brothers to grow up with and hugs and kisses and stability. And money. Lots of money to eliminate the problems the lack of that commodity would create.

She knew all about it.

As Cruise drove to the restaurant, Crystal was as quiet as Blake had become. Patty started telling jokes she'd read on the Internet and soon had them all laughing.

Cruise let Crystal and Patty out at the curb of the restaurant before parking the car.

"Crystal?" Patty asked as they waited. "Is everything all right between you and Blake?"

She didn't want to admit she didn't know what had gone wrong between them in the past half hour. Blake had retreated from her, cloaking his emotions so she couldn't read them. It hurt more than she thought possible, but she'd never admit it aloud. To admit something like that could do two things: show that she cared and cause an argument. Both were inadmissible in the kind of "non-serious" relationship she and Blake said they had. "Fine. Why?"

Patty looked puzzled. "I don't know. You both got so quiet all of a sudden. Cruise didn't say anything to upset you, did he? Sometimes he doesn't think before he says something."

"No." Crystal reached out and gave a squeeze to Patty's arm, warmed by her friend's caring. "We're fine. Honest."

But they weren't, and she knew it. Blake had retreated into himself and Crystal, for the first time since meeting him, felt left out in the cold. It was awful and so alone.

She wanted to shake Blake, to demand he tell her what was the matter. But she couldn't. She was even more afraid of his answer than she was of his silence.

BLAKE ESCORTED Crystal into the restaurant, his hand on her elbow. To the touch, she seemed cool, but in reality, his fingers felt as if they were burned by her skin.

Damn her anyway!

Listening to Cruise and Patty teasing each other had zeroed in on something he hadn't realized until just that moment. It was such a simple something that he shouldn't have been upset, but he was. Truths had a way of turning into a hammer and hitting the ego for not paying attention to begin with.

The truth was that Blake wanted to have a relationship with a woman like Cruise had with Patty. More than wanted it, he craved it.

Those quiet, personal intimate little pieces of information, the glances, the knowledge of knowing what the other was thinking, the feeling of being a part of a whole.

Until Crystal came into his life, having a steady woman wasn't an issue. Reticent and shy as a kid, he'd carried that same personality quirk into adulthood. He didn't know if it was because he was always physically separated by others because he was the son of a small-town minister and therefore, either supposed to be very bad or very good. Until now, he'd never bothered to give his past much of a look. He'd just accepted himself as he was.

For whatever reason, he'd never been close to anyone, especially a woman. He'd never had a problem with that before. Now, however, he had a glimpse of what being close to a woman was really like. What that connection was all about. Patty and Cruise hadn't invented it, but while being with Crystal it had been highlighted for him. What he saw between them was strong and sweet and kind and vulnerable and similar to having a best friend, a playmate, a helpmate and a lover for life—all in the same house. In the same bed.

And now that he saw it and knew what it was that he was missing in his own life, he wanted it.

And, dammit! He wanted it with Crystal!

WHEN DINNER WAS OVER, the four friends went to a nightclub where the music was a cross between disco and hard rock. They found a table and sat close to the dance floor so Crystal and Patty could watch the dancers. Blake followed Cruise's lead. He hadn't been to a club since college some ten years ago. It wasn't part of his adult life and there certainly wasn't a woman he wanted to pick up in this atmosphere. Although, as he looked around, several nice people seemed to be looking about, too. Good-looking women and lonely men.

One of them was trying to catch Crystal's eye, but she was so busy whispering to Patty she hadn't noticed yet. Blake gave a dangerous, narrow-eyed gaze at the man in question. He must have felt it, because when he looked at Blake and realized just how angry he was, his gaze skittered away from the table.

"Are you practicing mind control?" Cruise asked in a low voice as they received their drinks. "I'll tell you now, it doesn't work. Some jackass will ignore all the signals and try anyway. You've just got to trust her, Blake."

"I do. It's the other guys I don't trust," he stated grimly.

"You won't get her that way. Crystal doesn't look like the type to put up with anything that smells like a leash. Or jealousy."

Blake reached for his beer and took a draw. "She has so far."

"Yes, but that's because you haven't asked for more."

He was irritated. That remark smacked of his problem. He wanted more from Crystal. He just wasn't sure how much more or where to draw the boundaries. "How'd you get so smart?"

"By watching my friends make asses out of themselves and then asking Patty what went wrong."

"And she tells you? Don't you know yourself?"

Cruise gave a laugh. "I'm not into all the dissecting, man. That's not my thing. But she tells me what the women have said, and I know what the guys have said. Funny thing is that it's never the same. We men don't seem to see the problems as well as the women who voice them."

"Really?"

"Really."

"What has Crystal said?"

Cruise laughed. "Oh, no, I'm not doing your homework for you. You've got to ask her for yourself. Find out as much as you can."

"Easier said than done," Blake stated glumly.

Crystal was gathering more attention as they watched. Her long blond hair hung loosely down her back, and her figure was more full than some of the Ally McBeal clones standing around. Her large brown eyes circled the room as she and Patty dissected the women's clothing. They seemed to be everywhere but on him. Once in a while she'd glance over and smile, but she had retreated from him as he had done earlier.

She had a beautiful face, but usually that put off many men who weren't eager to get to close to a beautiful women. It was her expression that drew the men. He knew it. Crystal had a way of looking as if she was having fun all by herself. Men liked that. They wanted to be part of the excitement.

Another man from the dance floor winked at her, and she smiled at him, too.

Damn!

"Let's dance," he growled, surprising everyone as he pushed back his chair.

Crystal gave a surprised look, but stood and walked in front of him to the parquet floor. Instead of jiggling around the floor to the fast music, Blake did what he wanted: he divided the beat in half and took her securely in his arms and danced...slowly.

Her gaze gleamed in only a few seconds of pleased shock before she smiled slowly, clasped her hands around his neck and curled her soft body into the hardness of his chest. Her head rested between his neck and shoulder. Perfect. With a possessive touch and satisfied sigh, Blake wrapped his arms around

Crystal and swayed to the music, oblivious of the glances—both puzzled and jealous—that came their way.

Now things were the way they were supposed to be. And the rest of the world could go find their own dates and desires. This frustrating, exasperating, wonderful woman was his.

CRYSTAL STOOD in the doorway of Blake's kitchen and watched him pour two glasses of ice water into goblets. "You're sure this is what you want?" he asked, handing her one.

"I'm sure."

He came around the doorway and faced her. "Tell me what's on your mind."

"Nothing," she said, but her fingers splayed across his white shirt, the heat of his chest practically burning her hand. She was trying to find the words she wanted to say—needed to say. She wanted their relationship to change but wasn't sure how or what she needed to make everything all right again. She was running scared and needed distance or maybe time to figure out where her life was going.

"Crystal," he said, drawing out her name and telling her he knew she was lying.

She was reluctant, but she took a deep breath and asked the question that was on her mind anyway. "Did you bring me back here to make love to me, then take me home?"

He hesitated. "Yes."

"An honest answer," she said, disappointed and not knowing why, either.

"Why? Don't you like that idea?"

She told herself to stay as honest as she could. It was important that be up-front with Blake. "I don't know. I feel as if our making love is expected."

Blake looked surprised. "Do I treat you that way? Take you for granted?"

"No, of course not, but I think we're getting, uh—" she grasped at words that would explain the panic that flooded her with adrenaline "—too comfortable with each other."

Blake looked stunned. "Comfortable?"

"I think so," she said, grateful she'd said anything that made sense.

Blake carefully placed his glass on the counter. His gaze narrowed as if he were examining her very soul. "Let me get this straight. You think that we've gotten too comfortable with each other so you want to call this relationship off."

"I just think we need to pull back a little," she explained, but it sounded weak. Unstable. She was so scared. Blake was getting too close to her heart and if she didn't take care, she could fall in love in a heartbeat. She couldn't do that without giving up all her dreams—dreams she'd shaped her life around.

For the first time Crystal realized just how unusual her fears were. Although this was only the second relationship she'd ever had, this wasn't the first time she tried to retreat from someone who was getting too close. "I mean, I just feel..."

"...that if we weren't so 'comfortable' with each other, you'd still want to make love? Instead, you feel we're like an old married couple. Is that it?" he asked.

"Wait," Crystal said, imploring him to understand. "I don't mean it like that. I guess what I mean is..." She was at a loss. How could she explain her fear to the one person she feared the most?

But Blake sensed what she was trying to say. "...is that you want to run away, Crystal? Is that it?" There was a harshness in his voice that she wished she could erase.

"I'm not running away!" she exclaimed heatedly, denying his accusation. Whatever she felt, she hadn't gotten it across. "I'm standing here talking to you about it. That's not running, that's confronting!"

Blake stood, his expression closed. "Don't worry. I won't touch you, I promise. I've never forced a woman and I certainly won't start now."

His words pierced her to the core. She had betrayed what they had been to each other by her thoughtless words. She reached out, touching his sleeve. "Blake? Please, I didn't mean that."

Giving a sigh, Blake turned, not allowing her to back out gracefully. "What then, Crystal? What did you mean?"

She implored him to help her find the words to say what she meant. His gaze was harsh and stiff. And very puzzled. "What is it Crystal? What are you scared of? It can't be me, so what is it?"

She had to tell the truth. He deserved no less. "I don't know, but I'm petrified."

"And you want to run?"

With tears brimming, her brown eyes fixed to his. She nodded her head.

"Is it commitment that scares you?"

She nodded again. She was afraid to say the word out loud.

He smiled, but it was tinged with sadness. "Me, too, Crystal Tynan. Me, too."

"Why you?" she asked, bewildered. "You have everything. A stable childhood, a loving family. Friends. Why you?"

"I don't know where you get your ideas, woman." His anger drained, he sat once more on the barstool next to her. "I've come to think that no one comes into this world without some kind of problem."

"Some are worse than others," she said, still trying to sort through her confusing thoughts and glad he hadn't pushed her out the door and shut it in her face.

"God, don't cry, Crystal. I can't stand that." He tipped his finger under a tear, then took it to his lips. Crystal watched his mouth, fascinated as always with anything he did. Didn't he realize that was part of her problem? She was becoming *too* involved with Blake. Far too involved for her own good.

"Sometimes, Crystal, we make life even more complicated than it is."

"Really?" She tilted her chin in defiance of his insinuation. She was not making it worse, she was trying to be adult and not make the same mistakes twice. "And how *was* your childhood? What made you wind up so tightly?"

He grinned. "So you noticed."

A giggle formed in her throat, releasing some of the tension that held her. "A little."

"I was raised by a minister and his wife whose only purpose in life was to do good for others." He gave a sad smile. "I, however, wasn't one of the 'others.'"

Strange, his two sentences made more sense than five weeks of talking had. "Are they gone?" she asked.

"They're in Brazil on a mission." He hesitated a moment before resuming. He cleared his throat. "They've been there ever since the week I entered college. I think they were just waiting for me to grow up so they could leave without being branded uncaring parents."

Those words touched her heart. All those growing up years, he'd felt as alone as she had. She reached out and held his hand, bringing it to her cheek. The tears that she'd shed for herself earlier were now trickling down her cheeks for him.

"I'm so sorry."

"Don't be," he said, his other hand reaching out to stroke the side of her cheek and drift down her hair. "It's over and I'm a better man for it." There was a hint of self-deprecating humor in his voice.

"And I'm still whining."

"No. You have a right to deal with stuff just the

way you do it best, Crystal. Just like I have a choice, too."

"Just like, maybe you're still behaving as if you were a little boy being good so his parents will notice him?"

He sighed heavily. "I don't know. I don't look back."

"And I behaved like an outrageous outcast so my parents would notice me instead of being so wrapped up in themselves that all they did was argue all the time." She looked up, suddenly understanding another piece of herself. "I've looked at my circumstances so often that I overlooked the obvious, didn't I?"

"You're too complex for such an easy solution." Blake pulled his hand back while holding hers and kissing her palm.

Suddenly she wasn't scared anymore. She wanted more of Blake. Much more. Instead, he pulled back and stood. "Come on, it's time I got you home."

She wanted his arms around her again. She wanted everything to go back the way it was before she opened her big mouth without thinking things through. "Blake?"

He placed a finger over her mouth. "Don't say it, Crystal. Not now," he stated, his voice holding the edge of steel. "Not after all this."

"But..." she began.

Blake reached for her coat and held it out for her to slip her arms into. But his look said it all.

It said, *enough nonsense.*

Without a word, she slipped on her coat and walked out the door. She knew when she wasn't wanted, whether she instigated his reaction or not.

Within minutes, she was back at Aunt Helen's and she was whisked out of the car and walked to the door.

"Crystal, I..." he began, and she looked up at him, silently begging him to allow her to make mistakes without blaming her too harshly.

"I've never been in over my head before, Blake. I'm trying to stay on track. That's all."

He didn't say a word. Instead, he stared down at her as if his deep-blue eyes could eat her up in a thousand tiny bites. A deep-flowing desire flashed between them, taking away her breath with the intensity of their emotions.

Blake gave a low moan and slipped his hands inside her jacket, feeling the very curve of her waist as he pulled her to the lean and needy solidness of him. "Damn," he muttered before covering her mouth with his own, demanding she respond.

And she did. Her hands circled his neck and held on as if she were in the center of a swirling storm that had no end. She leaned into his body, feeling the heat and hardness of him and loving it.

His hands scanned her back and sides, finally running up her stomach to rest just under her breasts. After cupping them, his thumb flicked against one cashmere-covered nipple, his own moan joining with hers. She pressed even closer, rubbing herself against him, wanting him...wishing...needing....

His mouth ravished hers, telling her as no words could just how much he wanted her. When Blake pulled his mouth away, he gave a harsh gasp of breath. Her heartbeat pounded in her head, echoing throughout until all she felt was the pulsing of her body.

Dizzy. She felt dizzy with the need to be with Blake. She wasn't sure what to do. Heart and head, mind and body argued.

"Sweet dreams, Crystal Tynan," Blake said, withdrawing his hands from her body and walking off toward the car. He left her standing on the dimly lit porch, alone and wanting.

She watched him walk away, then went inside. As she got ready for bed, she felt sick at heart over what she'd done. She had truly messed up. And in messing up, she'd lost the one thing she craved...another night feeling secure and wanted, curled in Blake's arms.

Brushing away the window-decorating plans that littered her bed, she fell into the center of it and stared out the window at the brilliant stars beyond.

There were so few nights left....

10

BLAKE SAT UP most of the night staring out at his small patio with a stiff drink in his hand. Just one.

From the moment he'd met Crystal, he'd been intrigued. She made him feel a combination of excitement and comfort. Most of all, he felt real again, instead of hiding behind a facade nobody could get through.

Crystal took him out of that rut he'd been digging and made him see the world differently. Since she'd come into his life, he'd been doing things, feeling things, talking things, seeing things he'd never done, felt, said, or seen before. She was a magical combination of all the girls he'd wanted to date in high school and never had the nerve to ask, and the women he'd met who he was sure didn't care for him as a person as much as a ticket for status and income. But *all* those women had come after Blake as if he were gold on the ground!

In fact, this was the first time since he was a pimply teenager, he hadn't measured up to a woman's expectations!

What a blow to the ego.

He wasn't rich enough, didn't live in the right

town, nor did he dress well enough to look approachable.

It made sense that the only thing she wanted in her life was more money. Much more than he had. Short of robbing a bank, there was nothing he could do about that. He saved, but that wasn't going to add up to a million anytime soon.

That was one strike against him as far as Crystal was concerned.

Apparently, if Cruise was right, women had something on their minds that men couldn't understand. Blake was beginning to believe him.

Without the money being a factor, he and Crystal had hit it off in a way that was so special, it was hard to believe it might be over. He wondered where he'd gone wrong tonight, but it was pretty easy to guess.

As usual when he was with Crystal, it had been a perfect date. Okay, he'd known other guys were going to look at her in a way that would make him want to punch someone out. Because of that, he'd tried to control his own reactions early, and closed down a little. He thought he'd done pretty good, except that as he got quiet, so did she. Then they'd gotten to the club and he'd shown a little jealousy. But at least she hadn't made a big deal out of it. He'd learn to curb it. He was a big boy and able to overcome whatever he wanted to if it was within his power, and his own emotions were within his power. No one else's. So he had a little problem with anger. Now that he realized just how much he was in control of it, he'd handle it. It was that simple.

So jealousy hadn't hurt his chances with her. So, what had gone on in Crystal's mind that she would speak up when they reached his apartment? She had said no more lovemaking.

In the past five weeks they'd dated and then he'd brought her back here to his place, as if it were expected that she go to bed with him. Part of the payment for the evening.

That wasn't what he'd meant it to look like and had been a stupid fool for allowing their relationship to look like that.

From the very beginning they'd said this was just an interlude for them both. He knew it and agreed to it. He also knew that Crystal was so different from him that it would take a lifetime for the two of them to agree on more than a hop in the sack—although the agreements they had made there were the best in the world.

All this time he'd believed that Crystal was different—a rebellious, devil-may-care woman who had no problems with handling a casual affair with a time limit. When it was over she would be able to go on her way without a backward glance.

He was the one who suddenly wanted commitment and tried to conceal the fact—from himself most of all—that he was emotionally way over his head in this relationship.

He wanted something he couldn't have: a commitment from Crystal Tynan that said she would never make love to another man.

Fat chance.

What the hell was he going to do? He was crazy about her; wanted her in his bed this very minute. Didn't want to do without her and yet didn't know how to go about telling her so without having her run away now instead of before she left next week.

He knew one thing. If she could turn down making love to him tonight out of fear of becoming too involved, she'd never speak to him again if he made any move for them to become closer. Hell, she'd run fast and far, which is what she almost did tonight.

He had one more week with her. He wasn't about to blow it yet. All he could do was be friendly and available and most of all, he'd wait for her to make the next move.

Patience.

He prayed she would make a move toward him instead of away.

She taught him so much....

CRYSTAL SLEPT as if she were a babe. When Blake respected her wishes and didn't try to convince her she needed to be in his bed, she was so touched she wanted to cry. In fact, she did. His giving in to her without pouting or carrying on—much—made her want to take his hand and lead him to the bedroom for some of the most wild, in-his-face lovemaking he'd ever experienced—if she knew how.

Talk about feeling contrary!

She wanted him to leave her alone, then she wanted him to take her, then and there!

But Blake had more sense than she did. He'd stuck

to what she'd said and followed through all the way. And when he kissed her good-night then walked away, he left her wanting more of him than she'd ever wanted before.

She also knew he respected her enough to walk away. He hadn't wanted to, but he had. That put a smile on her face for the rest of the night.

He made her feel wonderful and feminine and very, very special. She'd tell him so first thing Monday morning.

Sunday she was taking Aunt Helen down to Phoenix to visit friends, and they would be gone all day. She wouldn't have a chance to see Blake until Monday. When she did, she'd tell him what she hadn't been able to put into words last night. She'd tell him that she had gotten scared because she cared so much, but that what she wanted most was to spend the rest of the week with him and celebrate their time together so that when they parted, there would be nothing but wonderful feelings between them.

Well, wonderful feelings except for the newly decorated window she was getting ready to spring on him. She was torn between believing it was the best idea ever to hit the streets or it was the stupidest, craziest idea ever to grace a window...

But she was doing it anyway.

If only Blake wouldn't get upset. She knew he'd be a little shocked. But she could handle shock. She just didn't want him to lose track of what she was trying to do.

She'd explain that failures are merely attempts that didn't work. At least she was attempting....

Crystal straightened her spine. She sounded as if she were catering to the man, for heaven's sake! That wasn't her role. Not in the least! They were going to walk away from each other as friends. This wasn't a lifetime commitment. She'd see if they could plan to have lunch together Monday so she could try to explain how she was torn between leaving and staying, but that she knew it was for the best that she leave.

AFTER GOING OVER the drawings one more time, Crystal just knew the shop window was going to be a success. She'd aimed its unveiling toward Valentine's Day, and would dress the window two days before the big event. Three days before she left.

Five days from now.

She had drawn up plans for it and had gathered supplies. Her Aunt Helen would laugh. Linda would be shocked but secretly enjoy it. Several of the mall walkers wouldn't realize what the window decor was, but those that did would get a kick out of it, even if they did think it was a little naughty. Or maybe *because* it was naughty. In the past five weeks, Crystal had learned that it was a myth that older people weren't full of fun. If nothing else, her daring window would bring in more customers just because they would be intrigued about the store inventory.

However, since it just barely bordered on the outrageous and might touch on some of the "rules and regulations of the window decor," Blake wasn't going to be too thrilled.

Gathering all the things she needed, Crystal placed her supplies in a box and hid the box in the storage room. She was having more fun keeping it a secret than she probably would have putting it together. Even Linda and Darlene didn't know what she was doing.

She was locking the storage room door when she heard Blake's voice coming from somewhere in the shop. Her heart skipped several beats. Although she'd slept fine, she was filled with doubt when she'd woken up. What if Blake was disgusted with her backing out of their relationship and didn't want to have anything to do with her? It hadn't dawned on her Saturday night, but it was her all-consuming thought this Monday morning.

"Hi," she said as he determinedly walked toward her.

"Hi, yourself." He stopped in front of her, blocking out everything except himself. "What are you doing for lunch?"

Doubt melted away. She smiled her best, slow, sexy smile. "I'm having lunch with you in your conference room."

His eyes widened for a moment, the dark-blue turning indigo-black. "I'm glad you understand that you have a date."

"I'll be there."

"And will you please bring your instant camera?"

It was her turn to tease. She gave him a sexy look

from toes to head before smiling. "My. Aren't you the confidant one?"

His chuckle was deep and dark and rumbled down her nerves like an avalanche. "I've made it a practice to never leave incriminating evidence or anything else you don't want seen twenty years from now, Crystal."

"Darn." She waited, knowing he would explain. But she wondered what the story was behind the lesson he'd learned and how it came about.

"I need a copy of something and I thought you could help me out."

"I had all kinds of interesting visions dancing in my head."

"Keep those visions," Blake commanded gruffly. "Just bring the camera." He bent down and placed a kiss on her mouth. It was too short and over far too quickly. "I'll be waiting for you."

Crystal nodded, then watched him leave. She moved around in a preoccupied daze the rest of the morning. Every five minutes she checked the clock on the wall over the door. Between Saturday night and this morning, Blake seemed to have found equilibrium in their relationship. Thank goodness.

Crystal didn't want to delve too deeply into her own reasons for feeling so relieved. She didn't want to put any more importance on it than admitting he was a good friend, and she didn't want to lose a good friend. He was a wonderful lover, and she might not be experienced enough to compare, but she was certainly smart enough to recognize wonderful. He was a grand companion, and she had never felt so complete....

Time to stop thinking. She was going off in the direction she shouldn't be going into, silently exploring areas that she shouldn't be allowed to think about, for her own good. But that didn't mean she wasn't eager for the clock to rush ahead!

Those two hours crept along, making her more nervous with each *tick-tock*. Finally, the time came. When she reached the mall office, she was more nervous than she cared to admit—even to herself. In the back of her mind was a drum tolling out the beat: five more days, five more days, five more days. She didn't want to think about what a hole her life would have once she went back home. It was too big to contemplate.

Marilyn was not at her desk. Crystal was disappointed. She'd gotten to know the secretary well over the past five weeks and enjoyed talking to her. Crystal placed a fresh daisy in the vase on the reception desk and continued into the hall leading to the conference room. Once there, she stopped, straightened the beltline of her black slacks and tucked in her gray blouse. Then she tugged at the short, matching cardigan sweater that ended at her waist.

Her knock sounded loud and she pulled her hand away as if the door were on fire. What was the matter with her? She was a grown woman meeting a man she thoroughly enjoyed for lunch. That was it. That was all. She pushed all other thoughts aside. Clutching the small camera in her hand, she knocked again.

"Come on in!" a voice called, and she did.

Her hand wrapped around the doorknob, she turned. There was a smile on her lips that wasn't there seconds before. If her acting skills weren't at their peak right now, they weren't far off the mark. She felt as if she looked stupidly bright and bubbly. A wonderful imitation of an airhead.

"Hey, there..." she began, but her voice drifted off as she stared around the room.

It was incredible.

A blanket holding pillows was spread in one corner of the conference room. A big bucket that passed for a wine cooler held a large bottle. Bright-colored plastic glasses and plates were spread out around a bucket of chicken and several types of salads. Large red-and-white-checked napkins were ready to use.

But it wasn't the picnic setup that was the shock. It was the rest of the room.

Ceiling, walls, tables and any other free space were filled with balloons—balloons of all shapes, sizes and every bright color in the palette. Pink and green balloons seemed to be floating on the ceiling while blue and black and white ones were clinging to the walls. Red balloons floated wherever they wanted to. Hovering over the large conference table was gold, silver and colored Mylar balloons painted with images of Snoopy, teddy bears, flowers, and all other sorts of kooky sayings and expressions. Each one was anchored with a ribbon and a piece of foil-covered chocolate.

"My word." Crystal tilted one or two to better

read them. Blake must have bought out an entire store of balloons.

"Hello?" She bent down to see if anyone was under the table. Blake?" she asked, looking through the balloons to find the usually rigid man who was responsible for all this. "Where are you?"

"Right here," he said, his voice right behind her ear. "We're closed for the day."

She turned quickly, and practically fell into his open arms. He reached for her, a little-boy smile on his face as he pulled her into his arms.

"What do you think?" he asked, placing a quick kiss on her mouth.

"That you're crazy."

He looked enormously pleased that she could say that. "And what else?"

"That you think this is sexy."

"And what else?" he persisted, still smiling.

"That I think I shouldn't be anywhere but in this room with you," she said softly, kicking the door with her foot so that it closed with a snap. Knowing what was inside, she dropped her purse to the floor just as she dropped the bombshell of her actions. "And that, in anticipation of this moment, I'm not wearing any underwear."

His blue eyes electrified. His arms tightened, making sure that she touched as much of him as his body could reach. "Well, now you're talking my language, lady."

"And that you're going to feed me, then tell me what it feels like to be buried naked in balloons."

"You'll have to experience that for yourself," Blake said, his eyes twinkling mischievously. "And we've got all afternoon."

Dismay filled her. "I have to get back to relieve Linda for lunch."

"No, you don't," he corrected, leading her toward the blanket. "I called Helen and she'll be there all afternoon. You don't have to be anywhere until the morning."

Crystal's eyes widened. "You told her what you planned?"

Blake looked so smug. So darn cute. "Yes."

She wanted to kiss him. All over. Instead, she pulled back and stared up at him. "What exactly did you tell her?"

"I told her I was going to make love to you on the conference table until you couldn't stand it anymore and admitted to me what color you wanted the ceiling painted."

That got her. She began laughing and he joined in. The sound of his laughter ran up her spine in delicious anticipation of hearing it again. It was such a wonderful sound! Blake didn't let go often, but when he did, it was the best laugh in the world.

"And then what?"

"And then I told her I was taking you on a drive, dining out and didn't know when we'd be back," he answered, and she knew that was the truth.

Going up on tiptoe, she kissed the side of his jaw, then allowed her mouth to drift by his ear. Her warm breath gave a light blow. "Thank you." she said softly. "Now if you don't mind telling me where Marilyn is, I'd appreciate it."

Blake bent down and whispered in her ear the same way she did his. "Marilyn has the afternoon off. Dentist appointment. The phone is plugged into the answering service because I'm gone for the day." He kissed the side of her cheek before nuzzling her ear. "So, it's just you and me, babe."

"Blake Wright, bar the door," she said, suddenly so filled with an emotion she couldn't put a label on and was afraid to look at.

The light in his eyes was more bright than the sun, more electrifying than lightning. Blake's mouth covered hers in a kiss that lit up her heart, filling her eyes with tears. Her hands cupped his face and she held him as if she were afraid he would disappear.

But he was going nowhere.

Blake edged her to the carpet, showing her in the only way he knew how that she was important to him in so many hundreds of ways. This was just one....

LATER, CRYSTAL LICKED the fried chicken from her fingers. "Then what?" she asked.

Blake was on his side, leaning on one elbow as he watched her polish off another piece of spicy fried chicken. "Then, I told them I'd be in their office in New York for the nine o'clock meeting on Wednesday morning. It's a major department store and we can hammer out the contract with them there. Our attorneys are flying out and their attorneys are already there. It should be fairly easy."

She stopped licking her fingers and looked at him instead. "That means you have to leave on Tuesday night."

"Tomorrow night," he affirmed, reaching out to clasp a thick strand of her hair that covered a breast, like Lady Godiva. Brushing the strand away, he gave a satisfied groan and devoured her with his eyes.

She didn't bother replacing it. "When will you return?"

"Friday afternoon."

Her face was somber as she looked at him with wide doe eyes. "I leave for home on Saturday morning."

His gaze locked with hers. "Can't you delay it until Monday?"

She shook her head. "I can't. There's too much to do. Besides, Sunday is a very busy day at the spa. If I work it right, I should be able to buy stock from the tips I earn on that day alone."

Blake looked at her in wonder. "You and Patty," he said. "I should just hand over my money to you and let you manage it."

He was trying to distract her from the sadness of leaving. She played along, knowing she'd never be so distracted that she'd forget about leaving. But there was nothing she could do about it. "I couldn't take that chance. What if I did something wrong and you lost money?"

"Then you'd be in the same ballpark as me,

wouldn't you?" he said, brushing another blond strand away from her other breast. He bent forward and took the very tip of one nipple in his mouth, sending shivers of need through her body.

They had just made love. Crystal had felt sated...until he touched her again. Was Blake magic? Or was it that she craved being in his arms more than she craved anything else in the world?

She couldn't worry about it now. Instead, she dropped the remaining chicken on the plate, placed it up on the table and joined him in the middle of the balloons.

"What did you say?" she asked, leaving a hundred kisses on his chest, trailing toward his navel.

"I said I think I found the way to this woman's heart." His voice sounded hoarse.

She continued on her foray. "Oh, and what way is that?"

"Put the sexy lady in an empty room, except for balloons and her man, and feed her spicy chicken until there's nothing else to do but make love."

"Mmm," she said, her tongue circling his navel. "Sounds like a plan to me."

It *was* a plan. Blake proved it.

Neither one thought again about the trip he would take tomorrow. They didn't want to.

They remained in Blake's office until after midnight. Blake wasn't worried, the security team was on the premises, guarding them as well as the property.

When they finally dressed, it was with laughter

and just a touch of sadness. Crystal refused to think of Blake being gone all week, and she knew she couldn't succumb to worrying about it. That would be deadly to her and to their already tenuous relationship.

While she slipped into her slacks and clasped the belt she stopped and stared around the room at the balloons still there. They had had a popping contest earlier and only a few dozen had survived the thrill of their chase. The small bricks of candy he'd used as anchors bulged out of the side pockets of her purse. She had been quiet for the past five minutes, trying to find words that would smooth over their parting. There were none.

Blake tilted her chin up to his. "Talk to me, lady. Tell me what's going on in that complicated head of yours."

She batted her lashes and smiled. "Why, sir, whatever do you mean?"

He wasn't in the mood for playing. "You heard me, Crystal. I saw an expression on your face that clouded your eyes. What's going on?"

She gave a small sigh that seemed to fill the air with sadness. "I'm sorry. This has been too wonderful a day to mess up with regrets."

Blake was a persistent man. No doubt about it. "Talk to me, Crystal. What is it?"

She placed her hands on his chest, feeling the wonderful safety of his arms as he circled her hips. Being with him was the closest she'd ever come to a feeling of complete peace. "I don't want this to end."

"It doesn't have to."

She looked up, locked in his gaze. "This has been the most wonderful five weeks I've ever spent."

He smiled. "Ever?"

"Ever."

"What about your first dog?"

"Ever."

"Your first Barbie doll?"

"Ever."

"Your first car?"

"Almost ever," she corrected.

"I thought so. A bridesmaid. Again." His gaze was tender and teasing, and if it was possible, she cherished him more at that moment than she'd ever dreamed possible to cherish anyone at any time in her life. Suddenly, the image of this big, masculine, muscle-taut man in a bridesmaid's dress was the funniest image she ever imagined.

She couldn't stop laughing.

After a few minutes, Blake joined her. "Well," he finally said. "I guess I touched your funny bone."

"How did you know?"

"Hey, I'm as good as Sherlock. Almost." He kissed her forehead, then dropped down to her cheek. "I could do that all the time."

"Not from Flagstaff, you couldn't," she said, dismissing the possibility of what he was intimating. Besides, she doubted that he was serious. They both knew how opposite they were in the ways that counted. After all, they couldn't keep the world locked out of their everyday lives forever. It just didn't work that way.

Blake hesitated only a second. "No. Of course. You're right. But it would be fun if we did, wouldn't it?"

"It has been," she said, pulling away and reaching for her small sweater.

"The end."

She stopped in midmovement. "Yes. But we both knew it was temporary going into this relationship, didn't we?"

He didn't move—didn't deny what she said—he just stared. "What if..." he finally said. "What if you stayed and worked for your aunt a while longer?"

"I owed Aunt Helen this, but it's not enough money. Besides, she can't afford to pay me what my usual salary is. I need to get back to my own profession and enough money to invest—" She hesitated. She'd almost said the unforgivable. The part about finding a rich husband. Those words tasted terrible on her own tongue. She knew it had to sound awful to his ears and would cheapen everything that she felt for him.

"Stay. Please." Blake's voice dropped to a hoarse whisper. "We have something so special, Crystal. So very important. Stay."

"I can't." Her voice was dogged, her tone brushing him off as if it weren't even a thought. She knew better. She'd thought of nothing else since Saturday night, weighing it with everything else in their lives and knowing that the ordinary life they each led would die under the pressure of trying to live up to each others' expectations. Well, at least his expectations of her. She'd never be able to play the role he wanted a woman in his life to play. She wasn't the junior executive type and never would be. He needed someone more staid and responsible. More quiet and not quite so boisterous or outlandish. Not such a women's libber...

No, she was not going to cry. No, she was not going to cry. No, she was not.

"Blake, you're so special to me," she finally said. "Can't we remain friends?"

His own expression was so sad, it emptied her heart and made her feel as if she were hollow. "I doubt it, Crystal Tynan. But, for my own sake and sanity, I'll try."

"Thank you," she whispered. "Don't be sad. Please. When you think of me, I want you to smile. Every time."

"When I think of you, Crystal, I'll probably have an instant replay of you naked and eating chicken." He gave a slow smile as he stroked her cheek. "And that image will do more than just make me smile. Every time."

She didn't say what she wanted. She didn't say she prayed so. She was selfish enough to want this memory to be theirs and theirs alone for all time.

She knew she'd never forget....

11

BLAKE RECOGNIZED the truth now. It had taken this business trip to make him understand. This emotion stuff was so new to him. Compared to Crystal's emotional intelligence, his was at the kindergarten level. But he was learning.

He'd known the reason for his lack of concentration on business almost from day one. All he could think about was the cruelty of the joke the gods had played on him by dangling Crystal—uninhibited, sweet, Crystal—right in front of his nose, then not having her feel the same way about him as he felt about her.

Blake loved Crystal.

He loved her with everything he had in him. Still, he just didn't know how to convince her that they were right for each other when on the surface they weren't.

She was so easygoing and spontaneous and enjoyed dancing on the edge of life, immensely. Not like him. He walked the straight and narrow. According to Crystal, he wouldn't even *peek* at the side of fun!

But she'd changed all that for him. He woke up every morning wondering what he was going to do differently this day. She made life exciting. She made it fun. She made it a challenge.

But his life was not any of those things without Crystal.

He'd rushed to the airport to catch the red-eye flight to get back a day early and first thing in the morning. Instead, he'd been shuttled onto another flight and was irritated to arrive late morning. His change of plans included dropping papers on Marilyn's desk, then going over to Helen's to enlist her help in convincing Crystal she needed to stay. Fat chance.

The stores were due to open any minute. By the time he got to the mall, he was in a black mood. He strode in and headed for his office, head down. It wasn't until he passed Helen's storefront that he realized something else had been changed.

The window.

Blake was almost afraid to look. Then he realized he couldn't. The mall-walkers were blocking it again. But this time, there were even more of them.

He worked his way to the front, then stared, open-mouthed.

The window background was draped from floor to ceiling in yards and yards of crumpled red and white lace fabric.

But that certainly wasn't the draw.

Perched on every available level, each one an eye-catcher in itself, were beautiful bowls, containers and accessories that the store was noted for. One was even a small red fan giving a gentle breeze to the items in the window.

But that wasn't the draw, either.

Music filtered through the window, romantic wonderful waltz tunes.

But that wasn't the draw, either.

The window centerpiece was a six-or-seven-foot gold-painted tree limb acting as a miniature tree itself. From each limb, as if decorated for Christmas—or Valentine's Day—were colored and gold and silver foil-wrapped decorations dancing softly, defiantly, in the fan's wake. It took a moment for him to realize exactly what those unusual but delightfully dancing decorations were. But the giggles and laughter coming from the mall-walkers gave it away. Blake narrowed his eyes and stared.

She didn't. She wouldn't.

Yes, she had. She really had done it this time.

Condoms. Condoms in every color and shaped individual package available.

Below, facing the customers, was a small, gothic-printed sign. Its simplicity took his breath away.

Show Your Caring By The Way You Love Your Sweetheart.

That was the draw.

Blake felt his frustration flare into anger. Pure unadulterated anger. How dare she flaunt something so...so...sexual and against the rules! It was one thing to talk and play behind closed doors. But to shove this under customers' noses as a reminder was absolutely forbidden. Who in the hell was she to do something so contradictory to what the mall's contract stood for? Everyone had an opinion on something but not everyone put it in the window!

One of the young girls standing beside him turned to her boyfriend. "Told you you didn't care!" she whispered accusingly.

"I didn't think," he said defensively, also whispering.

"That's the whole point," the young teenager sniffed before walking off. Her boyfriend wasn't far behind.

It didn't matter that it was tastefully done. It was one of the most eye-catching windows he'd ever seen, but he couldn't let it stay. It was too controversial. It was in bad taste.

It was Crystal all over. Controversial. Stating an opinion and meaning it from the bottom of her heart. Standing by convictions. Giving others food for thought. Embarrassing him.

When he thought he'd been totally outrageous decorating the conference room with balloons she'd topped him, and how!

He saw red, and only a little of it was coming from the direction of the window.

Just then, Crystal walked out. Her smile lit up her face when she saw him, but he didn't want to notice that. Her eyes danced with merriment and he took it as a slap to his conservatism.

"You're back early," she said, standing on tiptoe to give him a kiss. Blake backed away, efficiently brushing off her greeting. He had to keep his distance or he'd explode. "I took the red-eye so I could see you before you left."

"I'm glad," she said, uncertain as to what the matter was. Her hand rested on his arm. "Have you seen the window, yet?"

He stared at her disbelievingly. My, God, she was *proud* of it. "It has to go." His mouth was stiff. "It has to go now."

She stared at him blankly. "Go? Go where?" She glanced back at the crowd standing in front of the window, then at the customers walking into the store. "Why?"

"It's against mall policy. Get rid of it. Now."

Suddenly she caught on. He knew her by stance, and the look in her eye. "Against mall policy?" she said softly. "I admit, it's a little risqué, but it hasn't offended anyone yet."

"It offends me. Get rid of it now. This hour."

She straightened as if her spine were made of a broomstick. Her hand dropped to one side. "I've had compliments from a dozen store managers—all wanting me to create something equally striking in their windows—and you're telling me it offends you and it has to go?"

"Yes. Now." The blood was staining his face a dull red but he couldn't stop. How dare she flaunt sexuality that way? Why in the hell couldn't she keep it under wraps like everyone else? "I mean it, Crystal."

"That window has been dressed this way for three days, Blake." She crossed her arms over her breasts, and the sweater highlighted her curves. "It has received nothing but compliments. If you want me to change it, you'll have to wait until I return. I'm not doing it now."

He couldn't seem to stop his wayward mouth. "I want it done by the end of the day. It's disgusting," he snarled in a harsh voice.

"No, it's not." Her gaze narrowed. Now she was just as angry as he was. "It's just scary to your narrow mind, Mr. Wright. That's all. Well, grow up. Making love on Valentine's Day is a fact of life."

She turned and stormed back into the store.

Blake cursed under his breath, watching her move through the doorway. She smiled at a customer who stopped her and asked a question, then she disappeared.

There was a sinking feeling in the pit of his stomach. He hadn't handled this well at all. He wasn't sure what he should have done differently, but it wasn't what he had done.

CRYSTAL LEFT two days early. What was the sense of sticking around? If Blake didn't want their last days to be together, then she might as well get the hell out of Dodge—uh, Flagstaff. Aunt Helen drove toward the airport with a silent Crystal beside her. Her cast had been removed four days ago, but she was a little afraid of using her arm. The doctor had been adamant about her doing little exercises and forcing herself to reach for things, write or lift her arm above her head to brush her hair. Instead, Helen had a tendency to keep it by her side as if it were still broken. Driving was proving to be good exercise.

"Don't favor it," Crystal warned softly.

Her aunt never glanced her way. "I'm not. I just won't allow it to turn the wheel by itself."

Another two or three moments of silence went by. Crystal read each and every sign they passed. It kept her mind off Blake.

"If Blake could have been here, he would have." Helen's voice broke the silence. "He loves you, Crystal. He just needs some time to get used to you."

"He's now got all the time he needs. I never want to see him again."

"That's why you're leaving early, isn't it? Not because your boss called, but because you don't want to see him."

Crystal sighed. "I'm sorry, Aunt Helen. But there's no sense rehashing this. He can't control his temper or his thoughts and I'm not his mommy or his teacher."

"We are all in some way, darling. You were teaching him and learning from him."

She pressed her hands into her thighs until her palms hurt. "I know."

"I thought..." Helen began.

Tears sprang unbidden in Crystal's eyes, but she refused to allow them to fall. Instead, she read another sign out the car window. "I know."

"Then, why..."

"Because this incident just underscored why Blake isn't what I need for happiness."

"Darlin' you're wrong," Helen said firmly. "I know your goals. We've talked about them before. But you need to be flexible, Crystal. Goals change as circumstances change, honey. Blake is good for you, as good as you are for him."

"Maybe he might have been if he hadn't been so prudish. But then, if I had overlooked his puritan streak now, and gone for it, I might have made the biggest mistake of my life."

"I doubt it."

Crystal faced her aunt. "Did *you* think the window was offensive?"

"No, of course not. I wouldn't have left it up if I had."

"Well, neither did I. This highlighted just exactly why Blake and I couldn't be together for the long haul. We don't fit."

"I don't know that, and neither do you," her aunt stated calmly.

But Crystal was feeling every emotion in her body, tumbling one over the other in agitation. "What would have happened if I had given in to my emotions? I would have lost the dream I've been working for, that's what," she said, answering her own question. "When the bills for braces, football, costumes, cheerleading uniforms and all that other stuff are due, will he have learned to be calm? Would Blake be good then? Would he be willing to go without for the sake of children? Will he make enough money to allow me to stay home and manage the household and family we made together?"

"You've already got him walking out the door of your marriage because he can't cope with children." Helen tried to joke, but it wasn't easy. "A big part of life's triumphs is finding solutions, honey."

Crystal could barely keep herself in check and her aunt knew it. "Since there was no marriage, I don't have him doing a darn thing!" She shook at the very thought. "And since I don't have any more time, there is nothing else that needs to be said about Blake Wright." It was said more sharply than she first realized.

A wave of frustration and sadness washed over Crystal. This was the woman who was her mother's twin, who helped raise her and showed her how to be humorous and face the world. Who taught her individuality. And this problem of money—or the lack of it—was part of Crystal's problem. Facts were facts and needed to be faced. Her aunt had done that all her life and expected no less from her niece, whom she'd helped raise. And one look at the older woman told Crystal her words had stung. She reached over and squeezed her hand lightly.

Her aunt was persistent. "You love him."

Crystal could deny it until cows flew. It wouldn't change a thing. "Yes."

"Then why not..."

"No."

Helen sighed. "I love you dear, but you are so very stubborn. We have never talked about your mother and her fascination with money. It was almost as strong as her fascination with your father. And now here you come, almost as stubborn as your mother was when she decided to marry your dad."

Aunt Helen never mentioned her sister in conjunction with Crystal's father. As a youngster, Crystal couldn't bear talking about her parents without bursting into tears, so in time it became a subject best ignored by both of them. The family had never liked her dad and Crystal had adored him.

"What do you mean?" she asked warily. This might be the first time it was discussed, but it could be the last time, also. Crystal wasn't about to listen to a litany of her father's faults. She knew them well enough.

"It was as if your mother had never wanted anything as much as she wanted to marry Bill. Our dad was livid." Her aunt grinned at the memory. It was apparently funny to her. "Bill wore leather vests without shirts, drove a Yamaha motorcycle because he couldn't afford a Harley, and couldn't string a sentence together without at least two negatives. To his mind, *ain't* and *no* were both necessary in the same sentence."

Crystal looked stunned. Her father? Were they talking about the same man?

Her father had been the manager of a retail branch of a major, medium-priced department store chain. He'd worn suits and white shirts to the office and he'd worked hard, occasionally rolling up his sleeves and helping move stock—something she'd heard everyone was impressed with except her mom's side of the family. "*My* dad?"

"That's right." Helen kept smiling as she turned to drive up the wide boulevard to the airport. "But he changed all that to be with the woman of his dreams. And the moment your mom told him he was to be a father, he grew ambition like magic seeds growing into a beanstalk, working his way up from a clerk to the manager, one very tough step at a time."

"I don't know the people you're talking about," Crystal said, remembering her mother's family always discussing her dad as if she couldn't hear. Nothing good was said. "At least not the male members of that grouping. Besides, I thought you didn't like him."

"I didn't like him when he was changing. I told him to be himself." Aunt Helen wasn't stopping. She knew what her topic was and stuck to it. "Everyone who knew Bill before his marriage was stunned to see the difference afterward. Everyone but his own father-in-law, your grandfather, who didn't give a rat's tail about where he was going because your grandpa couldn't see how far he had to come to get where he was."

Grandpa. Crystal remembered remarks made by that old gentleman. And she remembered her mother echoing those same remarks on the way home from the quarterly visits to Flagstaff they'd made as a family. How hard it must have been for her dad to be put down so constantly in front of his wife and daughter—and all because he hadn't made enough money. But it wasn't just that. Her grandfather had said he didn't fit in, whatever that meant.

"I remember some of that," she finally admitted.

"Then if you do, you know that your father said that if they could ever live within their means, they'd be rich indeed. And that it wasn't that he didn't make enough, it was that they spent too much." Helen laughed. "Poor Bill. He was on the right path of logic, but no one appreciated it. Especially not his father-in-law."

Crystal didn't say anything for a little while, unwilling to let Aunt Helen have the satisfaction of knowing that her message had hit home. But still, for her family, money had been a major problem. It always brought arguments that had lasted late into the night. That didn't change things. And Crystal wasn't dumb or blind to what money could have done for her if she'd had some while going to college. But it hadn't been there, and she'd survived. She just didn't survive with a college diploma.

She said the only words she knew would stop the mental and emotional debate. The same ones that stopped the fear. "I can't."

"It's certainly up to you, and I wouldn't begin to tell you how to live your life. I love you too much." Helen pulled up to the curb of the airport's departure area. "Besides, I can't be responsible for your happiness. I can only hope for the very best, say what's in my heart and trust you to make the right decisions for you."

Leaning over the seat, Crystal kissed her aunt on the cheek. Tears pushed at her eyelids but they weren't going anywhere. She was in charge. "I might not thank you for all you've done for me. But in my heart, I say so every day," she said, her voice thick with emotion. "I know you're looking out for my interests, but this time..." she hesitated, unable to put into words what she wanted to say.

Her aunt did it for her. "This time you've decided to remain stubborn instead of following your heart."

Crystal closed her heart to the words. "I know what's good for me."

"Well, you're wrong."

Tears burned her eyes. A horrible empty pain invaded her heart. She wanted to defend her decision to leave, but this wasn't the time and place and suddenly she couldn't think of the right words. "You know my parents and you can say this?"

"My sister was a wonderful woman and I loved her. But I wasn't blind, Crystal. When it came to our dad, she was a fool. She'd try to please him no matter what the expense to herself and her family."

Crystal felt tears forming again. "Please. Don't do this. Please." It sounded like begging. It was.

Her aunt's sigh echoed through the car interior despite the traffic noise surrounding them. "I give up, Crystal. I think you're sending the best thing that ever happened to you down the pike. However, it's not my life and I can't interfere any more than stating my opinion." She gave her niece a hug. "But I love you with all my heart. Just as if you were my own daughter. And I pray you realize the mistakes you make before you can't correct them."

Crystal stood firm. She had to or she'd break down

right here, in front of her aunt. "This decision is right for me," she said, returning the gesture. "I'll be fine." Her smile was forced. She gave her aunt a kiss on the cheek. "I'll call when I get home and I'll e-mail once a week. I promise."

When she slipped out of the car, Crystal reached in the back seat for her suitcase and headed toward the airport's sliding doors.

Her feet felt like lead weights.

Most horrible of all, the tears she'd tried to keep at bay refused to do her bidding. They quietly streamed down her cheeks and plopped on the front of her sweater.

The flight attendant gave her an odd look, but didn't question, thank goodness. All the way back to Albuquerque—an hour by air—Crystal sat quietly staring out the window, wishing that she could settle for less than her dream.

If wishes were horses, then beggars would ride, her dad had used to say wearily to her mother as she'd succumbed to nagging him about something inevitably instigated by her grandfather. That weary expression of her father's was imbedded in her brain, as were many of her grandfather's comments—all of which had to do with money. The lack of funds had been a problem since she was born, apparently. This was the first time she'd realized just how far back the problem went. Aunt Helen had just shown her that. No wonder Crystal had formed a relentless relationship with money.

But it was her life. She had to choose whatever made her happy.

An image of a smiling, sexy Blake popped into her head and she pushed it away.

She'd get through these next few weeks and then she'd be over the worst of this emotional turmoil. Then maybe she could see her fling with Blake as nothing more than a grand adventure.

Crystal stared out the window as the plane landed and headed toward the bay. She knew she was imagining things, but she thought she saw Blake standing at the window and waving. It couldn't be Blake. He wasn't there.

Apparently, she was worse off than she thought. Damn the tears…they returned.

CRYSTAL SPENT the next couple of days in a blue funk. She was just out of step with her job, that was all. The creative fun of decorating windows was over and she missed it.

She also missed Blake in her life. She wasn't about to deny that. He was fun and interesting and intriguing and sexy as all get-out. He'd been her intimate companion. She considered herself lucky to have his company in Flagstaff and knew that most of this funk she was in was because he wasn't with her. She had to occasionally remind herself of the look on his face as he told her what to do about the window. She had a tendency to forget that look…but it broke her heart to remember. Just the thought of living with a man who would try to manipulate her with anger was enough to send chills down her spine.

But despite all that, she knew she'd have to admit one more thing: she loved Blake Wright with all her heart and soul.

She also knew she had to get over him or she'd never be able to have a life. Every time she'd be introduced to an eligible bachelor, he wouldn't be as nice, as sexy, as sweet, as good-looking, as much fun or as loving as Blake. It didn't matter whether or not he had a million dollars or more. He wasn't Blake.

CRYSTAL WAS A WRECK. Her heart and her head had seesawed back and forth so much she felt as if she were a chopped log. One moment she told herself to get over him. The next moment, she was crying because she was so lonely without him in her life.

With unshed tears in her eyes and determination in her head, she went to work. Valentine's Day loomed in front of her. At one time she had imagined just for a little while, that she would stay with her Aunt Helen and spend it with Blake.

"Three appointments," Tim, the spa manager, called to her as she came into the office area and placed her purse inside the locker. "One guy is in your room now."

"Thanks," Crystal said as she signed in and glanced at the schedule. "Half hour or full hour?" she asked with a frown.

"This one booked two hours."

"He must be a glutton."

"Could be. He looks like a weight lifter." Tim shoved the paperwork toward her. "Two more after him."

"See you in two hours," Crystal said, determined to remain cheerful despite the dark cloud over her head. A two-hour massage meant that someone had specific demands that would tire her own muscles out if she didn't pace herself correctly.

She entered the small room she used for massages. The lights were dimmed, two aromatic candles were lit, filling the room with lavender and vanilla, her favorite combination. Carl must have started the stereo and turned it low. It was at the beginning of a Ravel piece. *Bolero*. It's beat flowed through the room like the slow undulating movement of lovemaking. Crystal wished there were some other music playing. This was too...sensual. She gritted her teeth so she wouldn't break off the music and disturb the client's sense of security.

He was obviously a weight lifter; his muscles were well-sculpted but not overly so. Her client was lying on his stomach, resting his head on his arms. Crystal couldn't see his face, but his back was beautiful, and his barely draped hips were...familiar.

Ravel's music began building to a slightly stronger beat.

"Blake?" Her voice was a whisper.

No answer.

"Blake?" Her voice was soft.

No answer.

"Blake?" Her voice got stronger.

Still no answer.

Her heartbeat quickened, beating in her ears along with the music. She had loved him forever, known him for such a short time and had been miserable without him.

Never had she wanted to touch someone as much as she did Blake.

She reached for his back, her hands feeling the texture of his skin. Blake. It had to be Blake or someone just like him.

Crystal closed her eyes. Her hand wandered across his shoulder blades, feeling the slices of muscle, the sides of his body, the layers of muscles that tied his beautiful body together.

"Mmm." Although she couldn't see his face, Crystal was sure it was Blake. He refused to speak.

"Well," she began, reaching for the eucalyptus oil. "If you're Blake, then you paid for two hours and I might as well get on with it. After all, you're a paid-in-full client."

His back moved up and down a few times. Was he laughing? "Well, in case you're *not* Blake Wright, I'll continue as usual," she said sweetly. "Normally I start on the front and work up to the back, but this time I'll just begin in reverse." She flexed her hands and poured oil into her palm, then quickly rubbed her hands together to warm the liquid.

When she touched him again, it was on his calf, with long stretching movements that rubbed down the muscles of his leg to his foot. Her thumbs ate into the ball of his foot until he groaned. Somehow this groan didn't sound as satisfied as the first two did.

Ravel's beat increased in depth. Her fingers separated his toes, rubbing each pad as if it were on fire and she was stomping it out. He groaned again.

"But if you *were* Blake Wright, I'd tell you that I missed you and wished you were able to visit more often. Especially since you weren't there when I left." Her fingers etched into his arch. The music became a little louder. He groaned again, but this time it sounded a little like a pained echo.

Crystal grinned devilishly. Although she knew they weren't getting back together, it was so *darn* good to touch him again! "And that the least you could have done was call sometime this past week. You could have said hello, if nothing else."

Another groan.

"You could have told me how the weather was...."

Groan.

"...or whether or not we're still friends!"

A sound echoed through the room, almost drowning out the rhythmic musical beat that was growing even more intense.

"Mmm!"

With the quickest movement Crystal had ever seen on her table, the man flipped from his back to his front, dragging the folded sheet with him. He sat up in one fluid motion, his hands reaching out to grab her arms and hold her in a grip that was firm but final.

Blake.

She'd known it was him. But to see him face-to-face, his mouth inches from hers, was such a wonderful surprise. "Blake!"

His grin was feral. "If I hadn't been me, you would have been trying to hurt a customer. Probably a millionaire customer. You would have goofed, Crystal."

She cleared her throat before speaking. It was a stalling tactic as she prayed her voice would return. "I knew it was you."

"How did you know?"

"I recognized your back," she said, her mouth just inches from his, her mind concentrating on watching his lips move. More than anything she'd ever wanted in her life, she wanted to be in his arms.

Blake seemed to have read her mind. Slowly, inexorably, he kept his hold on her and leaned back on the table, dragging her with him so that she lay directly on top of him, touching every part of his body. She felt the heat of him through her clothes and gave a light wiggle.

"And speaking of that window decoration," he said, his voice low, "I owe you an apology. Although I shouldn't have reacted the way I did, you have to admit it was outrageous."

"And creative?"

"And creative."

"And you liked it?"

"I can't go that far." He grinned. "But no one has touched the window."

Immense satisfaction flowed through her. The window worked, or he would have stuck to his stubborn guns. Her laughter, soft, low and triumphant, echoed through the room. She kissed him enthusiastically. His mouth captured and held hers, taking the lead and making her know who was the boss—for now. She felt all the frustration of their separation seeping into the air and disappearing.

Her hands, still slick with oil, touched his shoulders, then held his head gently in her palms. When he pulled away for breath, she gave a heavy sigh and rested her head against his heaving chest.

"I missed you." She had promised herself she wouldn't tell him that. But the words were out.

"Marry me."

Electricity zinged through her body. She stiffened and tried to raise her head, but he held it close to his chest. "What?" Slowly his grip lessened and she raised her eyes to look at him.

His expression was somber, his deep-blue eyes steady, pleading with her to listen to reason. "Marry me, Crystal. Please. Now. This week. Las Vegas or here or Flagstaff. Anywhere. I don't give a damn. Just marry me."

Panic ran through her body. Her heart broke with the yearning in his tone and mixed with her own rushing blood. "I can't."

"Why not?" he demanded softly. "What in the hell is wrong with marrying me? We have much more in common than you think, Crystal Tynan. So why don't you give up and marry me so you can start making *me* into the millionaire you think you need to be happy?"

"What do you mean, I think I need?" She grew indignant. It was easier than feeling this emptiness at the thought of him leaving and her going back to the loneliness she'd wallowed in all week long. "I told you. It's what's best for the children I'll have someday. To say nothing of having a husband who doesn't confuse his anger over a thing with his anger toward a person—especially if that person is me. You were angry with me for the window instead of just saying you didn't like the decoration."

"I'm sorry," he said, almost biting his tongue to keep from giving explanations. This was something she had to get off her chest. And he had to listen.

"So am I. I'm not responsible for your anger. You are. You deal with it however you want, just don't expect me to deal with it, too." Her chin tilted up. "I'm not your wife or your mother or your parent, although I think I could have been a better parent to you than yours were."

"Let's leave my parents out of this, okay?" he said, gritting his teeth. She was right and he had to learn not to defend his every position.

"What's best for your children is having a loving mother *and* father. Having values that don't equal money, because money is a flat bed partner." Although there was anger in his eyes, he grinned wolfishly. "Unlike me."

"We have nothing in common."

"Like what?" he asked, taking time to nibble on her neck and make her realize just how much she missed his touch. "There's nothing important that we can't work out."

She hated it when he was logical. Besides, she could hardly think over the noise of rushing blood in her ears. She thought it was panic, but she wasn't sure. Better to keep on target and stick to her guns, and know what was best for her—all that stuff she'd said to herself a thousand times before.

She raised her chin so he had better access. "You don't like people who like mornings. Like me."

"I'll smile more."

"You don't eat salads, and I live on them."

"I'll try them or cook something myself." He kissed the curve of her throat "I'm a big boy now."

She felt his body beneath her and knew the imprint of him against her would be in her mind forever. He was so perfect in so many ways.

"You live anywhere your job takes you, and I need roots like my Aunt Helen."

"We'll find a place we both love and live there."

She knew he lied. He was too ambitious to put his career on hold that way. "You love sailing and I get seasick."

Silence.

"Blake? No comment?"

"You're right. I love sailing and you get seasick."

"You won't give it up?"

"Nope."

She pulled back and glared down at him. "See what I mean? We're not alike at all."

"We're not supposed to be identical, Crystal," he

said calmly. "You and I have lived apart for many years. We grew up differently. We have different tastes. Coming together should be a blending of those tastes without losing the identity we strived to create all our lives."

"Damn you," she whispered, wishing he didn't make such good sense.

"I love you, Crystal. I love you more than words can say. I don't give a damn if we're not the Bobbsey Twins in likes and dislikes. It will probably be a blessing in disguise anyway."

"Maybe," she hedged. But she still felt panic in acquiescing. At the same time, she was afraid to lose him.

"So marry me," he said in a low, throaty voice, his arms tightening. "Come marry me and be my love, and live with me beside the sea—or Oak Creek. We can tell our kids how we met and I proposed on Valentine's Day." He grinned. "They'll love it as much as we do."

She grabbed what she knew rather than try to sort out all the conflicting emotions. Reluctantly, she pulled away from him and stood up. "I can't. I need to know that the needs of the family I bring into the world will be met, Blake. I won't put my kids through what I went through. The arguments about money spent and money saved and money donated and money used. My worst nightmares are made of those memories."

Blake sighed and sat up. "I don't know why I'm

arguing. You obviously don't care enough for me to see anything but what you want to see."

He was staid, conventional and on a life path that was different from hers. She was breezy and into a life-style that was foreign to him. Two years from now, he'd probably hate the very things he now loved about her. And she would hate that she hadn't found enough money to raise her children as an at-home mom.

"You don't understand," she said, tears filling her throat.

"Sure I do. You don't love me."

"That's not true."

Blake stared at her, waiting for her to say something else, but she couldn't—wouldn't—admit to anymore. Instead, she bent over her supply table and blew out the candles.

"Your aunt is a millionaire. Did you think that was what made her happy? Or was it your uncle? Or her life-style? Her work?"

She stared at him, stunned as his words sank in. "My Aunt Helen?"

"Yes. She had to show me her financial statement in order to open her shop six years ago." He brushed the information aside, as if it were unimportant. "But what you don't know is that most millionaires don't flaunt it, Crystal, or they wouldn't be millionaires long. Half the time they don't spend any more money than you and I would. They just live like ordinary people, doing ordinary things."

"Like you."

"Like I will be someday." The sheet dropped to the floor as he slipped off the table and stood, reaching for his briefs and pants. He was oblivious to the beauty of his body. "And I will also be a husband and a damn good father, too." He stepped into his briefs. "But you won't know that because I'll be somewhere else, married to someone else." He pulled up his pants, his gaze like blue ice. "Just like you."

"Blake..." she began, working around the hurt her heart was going through just at the thought of those words becoming reality.

"I won't say how happy I'll be, because you are the love of my life, Crystal." He slipped his arms into his shirt and buttoned it up, then tucked it inside his waistband. The shirt wasn't tucked in properly, and with anyone else it wouldn't have been noticed, but for Blake, it was so out of character she wanted to straighten it for him. "You are the woman I'll probably love for the rest of my life. But I'll try to make a go of my life in spite of that, and I'll be damned if I won't have what I need to feel whole and complete, too. Just like you.

"As for your goals, marry the damn millionaire. But when people grow up and change, they usually find their goals change, too. They become more realistic and in tune with what they really need instead of what they want."

"You've been talking to my aunt," she accused, remembering the same goal-changing conversation.

Blake didn't answer. Instead, he stood with his

hand on the doorknob. "I'm sorry you didn't see the best thing for you when you walked into the room. I did. But I'm not going to force myself on you or try to convince you otherwise. All I can say is that you've missed an opportunity that even your common sense must tell you is wrong—the opportunity to be the best you can be with a man who loves you with all his heart." Blake stared at her, his heart in his blue-eyed gaze. A sadness raced between the two of them, for the first time connecting them with something besides joy.

"Goodbye, Crystal Tynan. I love you, but I won't beg you. I have my pride, too. Once I walk, I'm gone. I'll begin building a life for myself with someone who wants what I have to offer. And I'll give whoever she is all that I've got. I'll take the chance at happiness because without taking the chance, I'll never reach it for sure. It's scary, but it's the only way."

Crystal hurt so badly she could barely breathe. She couldn't speak. She blinked several times, her breath caught in her throat.

With one long look, Blake opened the door and walked out, closing it silently behind him.

Ravel's *Bolero* had been timed beautifully, coming to a crescendo just before dying away. "Goodbye, Blake Wright," she whispered to the silent, empty room.

And with the words came the reality.

For two months she'd known what it was like to be connected to someone who was interested in her just for herself—faults and all. All her life she'd wanted a man who would help ease the ache of loneliness. It had been her against the world for so long, it seemed to her suddenly that any other way frightened her.

And why, after all these years, was she letting something she thought was between her mother and father influence what *she* needed from a relationship? Hadn't Aunt Helen given her a different perspective of that relationship? Hadn't she realized that her mom had wanted her father's approval more than she'd wanted her husband's love? Father and daughter had both wound up unhappy, making everyone else unhappy, too.

Just as she would, if she continued to follow her mother's guidelines.

And most of all, her love for Blake held all the rest of her fears at bay. She loved the way he talked, the way he walked, the conservative side of him that balanced out her own wackiness—well, most of the time, anyway.

Besides, it wasn't a millionaire's money that she would curl up to at night. It wasn't a millionaire's money that would kiss her fears away or hold her close when she had a nightmare or give her joy by standing in silent awe on the side of a mountain watching a glorious sunset.

It was Blake.

He might not have millions, but when he was with her, she felt as if she were *worth* millions.

If she put a price tag on all that, then it was plain: Blake was her millionaire. And wherever he was, was her home.

Panic of a different kind rose. She had to catch him! She had to tell him how much he meant to her! She ran quickly across the room and flung open the door. Then she stopped her forward thrust.

Standing across from her, leaning against the hall wall, was Blake. His shirt was still stuck haphazardly into his waistband, endearing her to him as much as his standing there. Hands in his pockets, he waited for her to speak, his brows raised in silent question.

"I..." Her mind was in chaos. She prayed he'd pick up the sentence.

He did. "You changed your mind and realized how much you love me and want to be with me?"

She nodded.

"You realized that we had far more in common than you ever dreamed to find in a mate? And you even like my friends?"

She nodded. A smile dimpled her mouth.

"And you decided that I had the potential to be a millionaire if I paired up with you to use the stock market to the best advantage and turn pennies into gold?"

She nodded, her smile finally blooming.

Blake opened his arms. "Then come here, my Crystal, and be my Valentine."

She stepped into his arms, enfolded in the safety of his embrace. Blake held her close, his breath warm against her cheek as he gave a weary but contented sigh.

"I was getting worried, woman." His voice was low and hoarse, showing doubts and fears more than his words did. "I thought you'd never come to your senses."

"You knew I would," she murmured against him.

"No, I prayed you would. But I didn't know."

Crystal looked into the midnight-blue of Blake's eyes, seeing the love for her there. She saw the truth emblazoned there. He was a good man—the only one she wanted. She knew then just how right their love was.

Crystal pulled away, her cheeks dimpling. "Come back and let's discuss the, uh, terms of this marriage."

His gaze lit with fire. "With pleasure."

Being with Blake for the rest of her life was worth a million dollars...even more.

Back by popular demand are

DEBBIE MACOMBER's

Hard Luck, Alaska, is a
town that needs women!
And the O'Halloran brothers
are just the fellows
to fly them in.

Starting in March 2000 this beloved series returns
in special 2-in-1 collector's editions:

MAIL-ORDER MARRIAGES, featuring
Brides for Brothers and *The Marriage Risk*
On sale March 2000

FAMILY MEN, featuring
Daddy's Little Helper and *Because of the Baby*
On sale July 2000

THE LAST TWO BACHELORS, featuring
Falling for Him and *Ending in Marriage*
On sale August 2000

Collect and enjoy each MIDNIGHT SONS story!

Available at your favorite retail outlet.

HARLEQUIN®
Makes any time special ™

Coming in January 2000
Classics for two of your favorite series.

SECRET VOWS by REBECCA YORK & KELSEY ROBERTS

From the best of Rebecca York's

43 Light St.

Till Death Us Do Part

Marissa Devereaux discovered that paradise wasn't all it was cracked up to be when she was abducted by extremists on the Caribbean island of Costa Verde.... But things only got worse when Jed Prentiss showed up, claiming to be her fiancé.

From the best of Kelsey Roberts's

THE ROSE TATTOO

Unlawfully Wedded

J.D. was used to getting what he wanted from people, and he swore he'd use that skill to hunt down Tory's father's killer. But J.D. wanted much more than gratitude from his sassy blond bride—and he wasn't going to clue her in. She'd find out soon enough...if she survived to hear about it.

Available January 2000 at your favorite retail outlet.

HARLEQUIN®
Makes any time special ™

Temptation

A spicy hot love story

BLAZE

Available in February 2000

IN TOO DEEP

by
Lori Foster
(Temptation #770)

Charlotte (Charlie) Jones was used to fighting for what
she wanted, and she wanted Harry Lonigan—big-time!
But the sexy P.I. was doing his best to deny the steamy
attraction between them. Charlie was the daughter of
his best friend and father figure so, to his mind, she
was off-limits. But as he worked with Charlie on
an embezzling case, Charlie worked on him.
Before he knew it, Harry was in too deep.

BLAZE! Red-hot reads from Temptation!

Available at your favorite retail outlet.

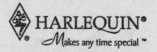

HARLEQUIN®
Makes any time special ™

3 Stories of Holiday Romance from three bestselling Harlequin® authors

Valentine Babies

by

ANNE STUART

TARA TAYLOR QUINN

JULE McBRIDE

Goddess in Waiting by Anne Stuart
Edward walks into Marika's funky maternity shop to pick up some things for his sister. He doesn't expect to assist in the delivery of a baby and fall for outrageous Marika.

Gabe's Special Delivery by Tara Taylor Quinn
On February 14, Gabe Stone finds a living, breathing valentine on his doorstep—his daughter. Her mother has given Gabe four hours to adjust to fatherhood, resolve custody and win back his ex-wife?

My Man Valentine by Jule McBride
Everyone knows Eloise Hunter and C. D. Valentine are in love. Except Eloise and C. D. Then, one of Eloise's baby-sitting clients leaves her with a baby to mind, and C. D. swings into protector mode.

VALENTINE BABIES

On sale January 2000 at your favorite retail outlet.

HARLEQUIN

Temptation

There are *Babies...*
Cute! Lovable! A handful!

Then there are BACHELORS...
CUTE! SEXY! DEFINITELY A HANDFUL!

What happens when our heroines suddenly have to deal
with *both*? Find out in the fun miniseries

BACHELORS & BABIES...

#761 A Baby for the Boss by Jule McBride
On sale December 1999

#765 Billy and the Kid by Kristine Rolofson
On sale January 2000

Come escape with Harlequin's new

Series Sampler

Four great full-length Harlequin novels bound together in one fabulous volume and at an unbelievable price.

Be transported back in time with a Harlequin Historical® novel, get caught up in a mystery with Intrigue®, be tempted by a hot, sizzling romance with Harlequin Temptation®, or just enjoy a down-home all-American read with American Romance®.

You won't be able to put this collection down!

On sale February 2000 at your favorite retail outlet.

HARLEQUIN®
Makes any time special™

Visit us at www.romance.net   PHESC